THE THORNING CEREMONY

A Prequel Humorous Fantasy Novel

THE WESTERN LANDS AND ALL THAT REALLY MATTERS

ANDREW EINSPRUCH

Cover design by Maria Spada of Maria Spada Design.

Editing by Vanessa of Red Dot Scribble.

Proofreading by Abigail of Bothersome Words.

Layout by Andrew Einspruch of Wild Pure Heart.

ISBN: 978-0-9806272-5-1

To Billie and Tamsin

Everything of greatest value that I've learned, I've learned from you.

AFTER THE SHAVING OF
MOLLUSKS

"Wait, wait, wait. Here it is!" whispered Princess Eloise Hydra Gumball III, tapping her reading pointer on her copy of the *Livre de Protocol*. "Scroll forward. The passage on the Thorning Ceremony is after the Consecration of the Sumps and before the Hoisting of the Silent Petards."

Her fraternal twin, Princess Johanna Umgotteswillen Gumball, glanced at their sleeping tutor, Master Thompkins Lyredog Overbolt, decided it was safe, and quickly rolled her scroll forward. "Got it," she whispered.

Eloise switched to the secret sign language that the twins had developed years before, anxious not to wake Overbolt. *Really, what is Mother's problem? Why won't she talk to us about this?*

I don't know, signed Johanna. *It's like she's pretending it's one of those antiquated rituals that no one does any more, like the Praising of the Royal Purple Cabbages.*

This thing is coming. We're turning 14 in a month.

The twins took a moment to read the passage. "Ye shall pierceth the flesh—scalp, face, neck, and hands—of the most honored maidens, and name from among them the Heir," quoted Eloise in a whisper. *Do you think this thing with the thorns is real?* She shuddered. *It sounds awful.*

Maybe it is a metaphor, signed Johanna. *Or symbolic. Like the Cleansing of the Upper Knowings. That was just a lot of smoke being wafted around.*

I hope so. Otherwise, it seems barbaric.

Johanna looked at Master Overbolt, who sat leaning back against the stone wall on two legs of his tilted chair, mouth agape, snores rattling his uvula, a drip of saliva dangling from a corner of his third chin, ready to join its fellows on the front of his tunic. Overbolt's mid-morning snooze overtook him like clockwork during their Protocols and Procedures lessons. *Should we wake him and ask about it? It might be worth it.*

I don't know, signed Eloise. *How likely is he to actually know anything about it? Even if he does, I doubt he could get through it in less than three days. I'm not sure I can stand more of his "tutelage" today.*

Eloise and Johanna had been taught Protocols and Procedures for the last eight of their 13 years. Normally, Eloise loved being in the Bibliotheca de Records and Regrets, with its shelves of scrolls and smattering of bound volumes. She loved reading, loved being surrounded by all that knowledge, loved the Bibliotheca's quiet hush, and the way everyone respected the assumption of silence.

But Protocols and Procedures dulled her enthusiasm for the place. Eloise had always found it hard. The straight-backed, cushionless wooden chairs in the windowless, candlelit study corner of the Bibliotheca were uncomfortable by design, to induce alertness, although Master Overbolt seemed immune to the effect. The study scrolls of the *Livre de Protocol* sat on angled stands, and they were never supposed to be touched, which suited Eloise—they smelled musty and were probably riddled with invisible mold. Protocols and Procedures lessons required a lot of sitting still (which Eloise detested), reading (which she liked), memorizing (Johanna was much, much better at that), reciting (ugh), and feigning interest (difficult when she, like Master Overbolt, tended to fall asleep, although she did not normally wake up babbling a string of non sequiturs).

Master Overbolt preferred rote memorization and extended monotonic diatribes over nuanced discourse or scholarly analysis. Eloise reckoned he was the dullest tutor of the dullest subject in all the four-and-a-half realms. The fact that his voice made him sound like an inebriated hamster with a lisp did not help.

For weeks, Overbolt had been forcing the girls to read, memorize, and discuss one of the most arcane passages of the *Livre de Protocol*, the List of Obscure, Infrequent, and Potentially Dangerous Ceremonies That Are Undertaken From Time to Time—a gathering of some of the most ludicrous procedures, processes, and rituals that Eloise had ever heard of. Over several weeks, they had covered everything from the Persecution of Bogus Affinities, the Tie-Dying of the Royal Smocks, and the Catechism of the Swamp Loungers, to the Exaltation of the Limpets and the Ululations Used Upon the Arrival of Minor Nobilities (Proper Forms Thereof). Overbolt's somnolence had given the twins a chance to search for something about the Thorning Ceremony, and at last, their search had yielded a result.

There's not much here, signed Johanna.

I know, agreed Eloise. *Normally a ceremony's every nostril flare and eyebrow twitch is described.*

With an unexpected snort, Master Overbolt startled awake, the front legs of his chair jolting down onto the stone floor. "Turbidity!" he exclaimed. "Malarkey, snool, diphthong, hemidemisemiquavers!"

Eloise and Johanna looked down at their scrolls. It upset him when he knew they'd noticed him sleeping during their lesson, and he tended to punish them by assigning outlandishly difficult passages to memorize. (Eloise could still recite from memory the 50 Indicators of Noxious Mustards.)

Should we ask him? Johanna asked.

May as well.

Overbolt wiped a hand across his face and peeked through his fingers to see if anyone had noticed he'd been off to the La La Realms.

Convinced he was safe, he tugged at the tufts of hair that sprouted like sheaves of wheat from his ears. He then tidied the corner of his mouth with a swipe of his thumb and middle finger, wiped at the wet spot on his tunic, and then looked at the princesses. "I'm sorry, can you repeat the question?" he squeaked, stifling a residual yawn.

"Of course, Master Overbolt," said Johanna. "We were just discussing the Thorning Ceremony, and Eloise had asked if you knew the history of the ritual."

"The Thorning Ceremony? Not the Shaving of the Mollusks?" His rural Southie lisp made the words sound like "theremony," "thaving," and "molluthkth."

"No, Master Overbolt. You moved us on from the mollusk shaving," said Eloise. He hadn't, but Eloise doubted he'd remember. "It was fascinating, though. One of your best."

Overbolt's nostril flared with a one-sided sniff. He rubbed a hand across his face again to erase the residual fogginess, then hefted himself upward and turned so his back was to the doorway. He put his hands into his robe pockets, elbows angled like a hockey sacking girder preparing to play defense. "Are you being impudent again, Princess?" he hamster-lisped.

Eloise widened her eyes in mock horror. "Of course not, Master Overbolt. It is as you taught us. The ritual intricacies of mollusk-shaving clearly have deep, resonant ties to the culture of Court and the broader history of our beautiful and enviable homeland, the Western Lands and All That Really Matters." It was close enough to the sort of thing he'd say.

"Humph. Right." Another rub of his bald head. "The Thorning Ceremony. It has been a while since I studied it." He cleared his throat. "I remember something about it having to do with thorns."

A voice came from behind him. "Perhaps I can help, Master Overbolt."

"Who in the name of Çalaht's bloated gizzard is..." Overbolt turned, ready to give the interrupter a tongue-lashing for barging in on his

4

instruction. He gasped, suppressed a squeak, and dropped to one knee with surprising speed for someone of his girth. "My queen."

ELFRICIAN ISSUES

T he girls jumped to their feet and curtsied. "Our mother, our queen," they said in practiced unison.

Queen Eloise Hydra Gumball II, Ruler of the Western Lands and All That Really Matters, wore a dress dyed deep royal blue, which had helped hide her in the shadows of the Bibliotheca for who knew how long. Her pale skin and the single diamond of her day crown caught the candlelight as she stepped forward, and Eloise wondered just how much she'd heard.

"I don't think Her Divinity would have had a gizzard, would she? Or is that a matter of Çalahtist factional debate, like the whole extended thumbs matter?" The queen's tone was mocking, but not unfriendly.

"No, Your Highness. It was merely an expression. And my apologies for—"

The queen held up a hand and Overbolt stopped speaking. "And here I thought you were telling me something that might needle the Venerated Prelate Herself. She's not easily needled, so it is handy to have something up one's sleeve. Oh well." She took three strides into the study nook, positioning herself between her daughters' chairs. "It is incredibly fortuitous that you are covering the Thorning Ceremony, as that's about to become somewhat relevant."

It was the first time their mother had made direct mention of it. *That's a change*, signed Eloise surreptitiously.

"I've asked you not to do that in front of me, Eloise. If you have something to say, say it for everyone to hear."

"Yes, Mother. I'm sorry."

"Carry on with your lesson, Master Overbolt."

Sweat suddenly glistened on the tutor's dome. "Yes, Your Highness. I was just about to allow the princesses a few moments to reacquaint themselves with the main text. Please do so, ladies."

Eloise wished her mother would stop by more often. Master Ear Tufts was never this solicitous when it was just the three of them.

Overbolt walked over to his own bound copy on a second stand and frantically turned the handles of the scroll, threading the hemp parchment from one to the other, searching for the right passage. He eventually found it, and grabbed his reading pointer—a superbly wrought silver rod that was 20 weak lengths long, with a hand shape at the pointing end, its index and middle fingers extended together, the ring and pinky tucked under the thumb near the palm. Using it to read gave the impression of a pledge being made, a vow to the sanctity of the text and the honor of scholarship. (More heretical sects used a reading pointer that only had the middle finger pointing at the page, but this was not spoken of in polite company.) The reading pointer helped ensure that oils, sweats, musks, or whatever the person reading might secrete did not damage the scroll, and helped keep them in a mindset focused on the task at hand.

Overbolt leaned forward, squinted, moved a candle closer, squinted again, then mouthed words silently as he sped through the text.

It gave Eloise and Johanna time to sit down and do the same. The queen stood behind them, back straight, arms crossed, tapping a folded fan in the crook of one elbow. The air in the small nook filled with a growing sense of impatience.

Overbolt straightened. "Right. Of course." He cleared his throat. "As is apparent in the text, the Thorning Ceremony dates to before the early establishment of the realms, and is a rite of passage that takes place around the 14th birthday, reserved for the highest-born of female nobles."

Johanna, lost in the scroll, began to giggle. A moment later, the giggle evolved into a full laugh. She looked up, realized what she'd done, and put a hand over her mouth to suppress it.

"Yes, Princess Johanna?"

"I'm sorry, Master Overbolt. I was just reading the Commentaries. I think Elfric the Elder and Elfric the Younger might have had, um, issues."

"Princess!" Overbolt gasped, scandalized. "It does not do for you to call into disrepute the Commentaries in front of our queen."

The *Livre de Protocol* was produced in various forms. Fancy bound volumes were large and sumptuously illustrated with text organized into pages, designed to sit open prominently in the middle of a rich person's drawing room. Others were written in very small hand, meant for carrying around when traveling. However, the most interesting ones, like these study copies in the Bibliotheca de Records and Regrets, were combinations of the main text and associated commentary—faithful duplicates of the one original scroll, which was held elsewhere in the building and guarded by zealous bibliothecarians. In these editions, the main text appeared in the middle of a page, and scholarly musings were written (or, in the case of copies, reproduced in something approximating the original handwriting) around the text, so the scholars' thoughts could be studied in conjunction with the words that had inspired them. Over the years, the original scroll of the *Livre* had come to look like a graffitied public facility wall, which made creating copies extremely hard. Eventually, scholars had called a halt to adding comments, and the *Livre* became a fixed document, with the commentaries cementing into the Commentaries. Now, anyone who wanted to opine on the text had to do it on a scroll somewhere else.

The queen stepped across to Overbolt's reading table and lectern, the tutor bowing his way a few steps backward to make room for her. She held out her hand, and Overbolt, after a moment's confusion, handed her his reading pointer. The queen used the silver rod to gesture at Johanna. "Would you care to enlighten the rest of us as to the nature of these Elfrician issues?"

Johanna took that as her cue to stand. "Of course, Mother. The first comment, which you can see in the upper left-hand corner here..." She indicated with her pointer. "It's from Elfric, obviously before he was Elfric the Elder and there was an Elfric the Younger. He talks about how the piercings should be taken literally, as a rite of passage for those who undergo it, a promise to those they might rule, and says that they should take succor from those in attendance. Then a few comments below, there's a first entry from Elfric the Younger, saying that it is 'easy to ignore the allegedly scholarly opinions about succor and the necessity of literal piercing from certain commentators who were never home and broke many a promise of showing a loving son the basics of hockey sacking. And if they can't do that, then their literalist words are dust.' Instead, he emphasizes the symbolism of the ceremony as what's most important, admonishing against the strictness of literalism."

"So, he's an interpretationist," said Eloise.

"Yes, Eloise. Let's allow your sister to continue, shall we?"

"Elfric, now noted as Elfric the Elder, appears again a few comments further down, emphasizing his position, saying, 'The words shall be taken as writ' and that 'one would be remiss to rely too heavily on remarks made by ones who do not give sufficient weight to the value of hard work, a roof over their heads, or clothes on their backs.' Then skipping down, Elfric the Younger has this longish passage about the 'richness and beauty of interpretation' available to those 'who can remove their heads from their posterior regions' and 'see shades of gray in such words as *pierceth*, *flesh*, *honored*, and even *maidens*, should one care to take off one's blinkers, being blinkers that blind one to the needs of those around them so much so that one cannot be bothered to put down a scroll even at the dinner table and join in the family conversation.'"

"And?" prompted the queen.

"Elfric the Elder replies up on the right here, saying that strong minds root their opinions on the words themselves, 'focusing on the piercing as rite of passage' leaving 'lesser minds to flounder about seeking interpretations,' and that any such interpretations can be safely ignored if they come from 'snotty-nosed brats who were constantly hectoring for attention day in and day out instead of fostering any kind of peace within a hockey sack's throw of them.' Then Elfric the Younger says something about 'not paying mind to scholars who wouldn't know good commentary if it jumped out of a forest and bludgeoned them with an axe,' and that '*pierceth* could be taken as *annointeth* if a scholar had any nous at all.' Then Elfric the Elder dismisses 'all comments from scholars who break their mother's hearts by staying out late carousing and making repeated, serialized, ill-advised choices for a succession of wives, which they were not able to keep ahold of anyway, and says that the ensuing description of thorns shows that '*pierceth* means *pierceth*,' and '*annointeth* means one should learn how to read.' Like I said," said Johanna with a smile. "Issues."

Eloise raised her hand. Her mother nodded for her to go ahead.

"Elfric the Younger seems to have the last word. The last comment on the lower right-hand part of the scroll is from Elfric the Only One Who Does Not Have Mulch for Brains and Who Can By Çalaht's Liver Cirrhosis Carouse When He Feels Like Carousing and How Dare You Speak That Way of My Beloved Alice, then Gemma, then Jemima, then Geraldine, then Elicia, and finally Trixie. He writes, 'Certain scholars can bite me,' which we can, I assume, understand as being taken from his interpretationist point of view, rather than his father's literalist."

"Right," said the queen. "I think we get the message. Or do we? Girls, what should we make of all this?"

Master Overbolt, who'd said nothing the whole time, timidly raised his hand.

"Not you, Overbolt."

He put his hand down, keeping an embarrassed silence.

Eloise raised her hand. "It seems to me the Elfrics Elder and Younger hit on the central issue. Would those who would have undertaken this ritual have done it literally or symbolically?"

"Not 'would have,'" said the queen.

Johanna blanched, but Eloise didn't see. "Pardon?"

"She means 'did,' not 'would have,'" said Johanna. "Or, perhaps, 'will.'"

Eloise looked at her sister, understanding creeping in. She turned to her mother. "This is not some antiquated, disused relic? This... this is real?"

"Yes."

Simple. Unequivocal. Eloise felt her mouth turn to desert.

"So who was right?" asked Johanna, her voice quiet.

"Oh, no question there. Elfric the Younger was an inebriant and an ingrate, and not a fraction of the mind of his father. Elfric the Elder was quite right. Gumballs have always sided with the literalist view."

"Always?" said Eloise.

"Always. I've received a message from the Thorning Master. She confirms that she'll arrive in three days. That should be enough time before your birthdays."

"Enough time for what?" Eloise felt her eyes watering. She already knew the answer.

"That's obvious, is it not? For her to prepare you for the Thorning Ceremony."

❧ 3 ❧

QUINCE JAM

"I'm sorry, Princess. I truly am." The servant, an aardvark who was one of the many people who took care of things around the castle, shook a little as she held the silver tray. "I can take them away, Princess, if you prefer."

Eloise considered the scones, then looked at the aardvark. Who was this one? Something de Aardvark. Judy? Lucy? Lucille? Lücy, maybe? Something like that. There were several of them, and many had a very similar look to their coats. She picked a name. "Lucy..."

"Apologies, Princess. It's Läääcy. Läääcy de Aardvark."

"Läääcy, then. What have I said about quince jam in the past?" She peered at a scone dubiously, as though worried it might sprout wings and fly off.

"I said it to Chef. I did, I promise. I said that you were not fond of quince jam and could I please have a different jam for you and that I would be most grateful if it could possibly be your favorite, blueberry, or raspberry, which is also nice, or at least strawberry. But Chef was not to be swayed. Chef said that she'd already deployed the quince jam and wasn't inclined toward waste. That put me in a terribly difficult position. I either had to bring you the scones with the quince jam or not bring the scones at all. I'm sorry, Princess, if I made the wrong choice."

It's not that she hated quince jam. Eloise liked it well enough. But she did prefer blueberry. Or raspberry. The girl was right, raspberry was nice. But quince jam was definitely much lower on the list, and now she was torn between sending the servant back to try again, and actually eating something. Hunger won out. "Well, do try harder next time, Lucy. Maybe say that my mother told you to, or something."

The aardvark's eyes went big at that, but she said nothing.

"But go ahead and put the tray on the table. I'll eat what I can stand to eat."

"Yes, Princess. I'll try to do better next time." The aardvark set down the tray and dashed from the room, closing the door behind her with a solid thunk. Eloise debated whether it was close enough to a slam that she ought to say something, but decided against it. She'd skipped breakfast, so morning tea took priority.

Eloise picked up a scone and took a testing bite. Actually, the quince jam was superb. Chef really did have a knack. Or a weak magic. Maybe both. Either way, Eloise would have to remember to move quince jam up the preference list in the future.

She poured herself a cup from the teapot. Haggleberry, her absolute favorite. No need for a list there. No matter what was going on, haggleberry tea always made her feel a little better about everything.

She had been thinking about the whole Thorning Ceremony thing since their lesson the day before. Eloise really wasn't sure what to make of it. It seemed like such an odd thing. She would just have to put it in the don't-worry-about-it basket. It would come up when it came up, and usually, there was a way around these things, even the ones where her mother came across all earnest and determined like she had yesterday.

There was a knock at the door—the rap-rap, rap-rap-rap, rap-rap pattern used exclusively by heralds and pages.

Eloise set down the half-eaten scone, stood, and smoothed her robe. "Enter."

A herald, a young hare who looked barely old enough to have progressed from page boy, stepped into the room. "Princess Eloise Hydra Gumball III," he said formally. "The queen requests your presence in the Receiving Room. She asked that you wear something nice."

"And?"

"Pardon?

"That was the whole message? Nothing about what 'nice' means in this context? Nothing about the purpose of the summons?"

The hare shifted nervously from foot to foot. "No, Princess. The queen did not share either of those things with me. Would you like me to ask her?"

Eloise sighed, conveying what she hoped was an adequate level of disappointment. "No, I suppose not. That will do."

"Yes, Princess."

The herald left, and Eloise quickly ate the rest of the scones and sipped down the remaining tea. It wouldn't do to keep her mother waiting. She rushed to find a suitable Court day dress, wondering who was coming that required the Receiving Room and a "nice" outfit. Well, never mind. She had other things to worry about. Eloise flipped open the trunk at the foot of her bed and began rummaging through her dresses. They'd been organized just the way she liked: by hue, using the same color pattern as a rainbow, although she did find one in the blue section that clearly should have been with the indigos.

She picked out a light orange dress from the middle of the precisely folded piles, held it up to herself, and considered it. No, it would not do for today. Her mother had called her to the Receiving Room, which meant the queen would likely wear something reddish or purple, and

Eloise did not want to clash. She tossed it on her bed and picked out another three possibilities, but none of them suited her mood. They, too, went on the bed. She didn't have much time, so Eloise pulled out all the dresses and slung them across her bed so she could see them all. That was the best way to consider her options. She didn't like having such a mess, but someone would tidy it up before she got back.

Deciding on a favorite aquamarine one, she walked to her door, opened it, and looked around. There was another aardvark folding linens in front of a linen press. Eloise didn't try to guess which one it was. "Would you please come here and help me dress?" Eloise turned back to her room, not waiting for an answer.

The aardvark followed her and helped Eloise into the aquamarine dress. She buttoned it and tied the sash into a bow behind Eloise's back. The princess checked the bow in her mirror and shook her head. "It's a bit crooked. Could you tie it again?" After seven attempts, Eloise was happy enough with the bow. "Thanks, that'll do."

"D-do you want help with your hair?" squeaked the aardvark.

It was a brave offer. Eloise hated having her hair done. Her curls were inevitably a mess, and all that tugging with the comb never helped her mood. "Uh, sure. Just a quick braid, though. I don't have a lot of time."

She sat at the vanity and braced herself. The aardvark separated her hair into three strands, and Eloise counted the strokes as the servant struggled to brush them, hoping for an even number, which she preferred. Nineteen strokes for the first one. An odd number, but a prime. Twenty-one for the second. Also odd. She didn't care for that. Eighteen for the third. Good. Plus, the "Ouch!" to "Be careful!" ratio was relatively low.

"W-what ribbon would you like?"

Eloise stood, grabbed out a handful of ribbons from the vanity drawer, found one that suited the dress, and set the rest on top. "This one, I think." She sat again as the aardvark quickly braided and tied her hair with the ribbon. The bow could have been better, but Eloise needed to get to the Receiving Room, so decided to let it be.

When Eloise said, "I'll take it from here," the servant curtsied and scurried from the room. Eloise tugged on a pair of matching slippers, tying their laces with precise bows in an orientation that perfectly mirrored the bow on the dress. She placed the hairbrush back in its spot, but didn't have time to tidy the ribbons. Whoever fixed up the dresses could do them too.

Eloise burst through her door at a run and slammed straight into an aardvark carrying a heaped armload of linens. The bedding went flying, the servant fell backwards hard, and Eloise barely avoided crashing to the floor. She spun to face the maid. "For the love of Çalaht, Lucy, watch where you're going!"

The aardvark groveled, gathering sheets and pillow cases as best she could at the same time. "I'm sorry, Princess. I'm so, so sorry."

"That really could have been a disaster, Lücy. I could have ruined my dress."

"I realize that, Princess. I'm sorry I was in the way. And it's Läääcy, not Lucy or Lücy, Princess."

"When you're done picking all this up, perhaps you could do my room? I won't be in there for a while."

"Yes, Princess. I'll do that."

"Good." That matter handled, Eloise turned and headed for the Receiving Room and whatever dullness awaited her there.

✺ 4 ✺

THE THORNING MASTER

Eloise and Johanna sat on either side of the queen, each on their respective thrones in the marbled coolness of the empty Receiving Room, doing something that Eloise could not remember her mother ever doing before—waiting. People waited for her, not the other way around. It made their sitting together even more awkward than normal, and Eloise tried to figure out what it might take for someone to have that effect on the queen.

Queen Eloise did not wear the Attention Cape, so this was not about grievances, justice, or entreaties. Nor did she wear the Tribute Cape, meaning this was not about tithes or the queen's percentage. Both were hung on the side wall, along with the Jangled Cape, the Obfuscation Cape, the Cape of Dashed Hope, the Disavowal Cape, the Bright Cape, the Elegiac Cape, the Really, You Don't Want To Mess With Me Today Cape, and several others, each with their own purpose, including one that was just there in case the queen felt chilled. Each cape set a tone for the meeting that was to take place, and the queen's choice provided a small amount of information to those who came before her.

But today, the queen was capeless. That made Eloise feel even more uncertain. She truly had no idea what to expect.

While she waited, her thoughts drifted back to the Thorning Ceremony and her mother's mysterious attitude toward it. The *Livre de Protocol*'s text and commentaries gave shape to the framework of the ritual—if you were in line for the throne and female, you got stuff poked into you and a lot of words were spoken. So, not an atypical Court ceremony, except for the poking bit. It also documented who might attend and what might be said. But all that was a hollow skeleton. Their mother was still silent on the topic, other than the brief encounter in the Bibliotheca de Records and Regrets. No word on what "preparation" entailed, nor what going through it was like. Nothing.

Eloise didn't think her mother was being secretive. It was something else. Distaste? Embarrassment? Both were out of character.

A herald poked her head halfway through the doorway. "Your Highness, she descends the main stairway and will be here shortly."

"How shortly?"

"Her movements are... deliberate. I estimate ten minutes."

"Very good. Please see her straight in."

"Yes, my queen."

Back to the waiting.

Five minutes dripped by. Long, increasingly uncomfortable minutes, punctuated only by small, inadvertent sighs from the queen.

"Mother," started Eloise, but the queen held up a hand to stop her. Eloise swallowed any further words.

A shuffle of feet mixed with the "tock" of a wooden cane became audible. Shuffle-shuffle-tock. Pause. Shuffle-shuffle-tock. Pause. Shuffle-shuffle-tock. Pause. Weak length by weak length the sound came closer.

"Finally," muttered the queen, and straightened herself on her throne. She clasped her hands in her lap and let her face relax to neutral. Instinctively, Eloise and Johanna did the same.

The herald stepped formally into the Receiving Room, cleared her throat with practiced exaggeration, and declaimed, "Baroness Sÿlvia Nûûûttëëërlïïïng Stúüübenhocker née de Gumball of Look Elsewhere For A Place To Claim Land You Intruding Amateurs These Hills Are Mine, the royally acknowledged Thorning Master."

A woman who looked old enough to have changed Çalaht's diapers shuffle-shuffle-tock-paused her way into the room. She wore robes of the deepest black Eloise had ever seen. Her silver hair, braided so tight it smoothed the creases of her ancient face, was a precisely coiled rope on top of her head, so neat and severe that Eloise doubted she could push a sewing pin into it. The old woman's cane, an ebony black enough to steal the light from one's eye, was gnarled and twisted like an arthritic menace and topped with silver cast into an eagle's clenched talons. But Eloise was transfixed by the dozens and dozens of thorns that she wore pierced through her skin. The old woman's neck, cheeks, nose, eyebrows, ears, forehead, and hands were riddled with all manner of thorns, from tiny thistles to massive cactus spikes. They poked into her skin, and in some places went through it. Most notable was a particularly long, purple one that sliced through a flap of skin between the corner of her eye and her temple. It was huge, three-quarters the length of her skull, and as thick as a drummer's beater. It looked to Eloise like she had a narrow aubergine poking through the side of her head.

Disconcerting.

And hard not to stare at impolitely.

"Hello, Little Elsie." She stopped, realizing her error. "Oh, pardon me. Good morning, Your Highness." Her voice was like stones crashing in a quarry. She slowly moved to the spot in front of the dais where the queen sat, and looked like she might be starting to curtsy. Eloise couldn't imagine how long that might take, but fortunately, the queen lifted an open palm, sparing the Thorning Master that effort.

"Thank you for coming, Baroness Thorning Master. You have arrived early."

"The weather was favorable. Congratulations on your ascension to the throne. I've not seen you since your Thorning Ceremony."

Eloise saw a slight reddening to her mother's cheeks. "Thank you, Baroness. It has, indeed, been a while."

"Your mother, may she rest in peace, was an unmitigated disaster as queen. I believe you might be somewhat of an improvement."

Eloise swallowed, waiting for her mother's wrath. No one ever spoke to her in such a slighting way, and the queen did not allow anyone to speak ill of her late mother, deserved or not.

Nothing. Clenched jaws, but no rebuke. Who was this woman?

"Baroness Thorning Master, it is kind of you to make the journey here to instruct my daughters."

Stúüübenhocker thocked her cane once on the marble floor, dismissive. "I would not be much of a Thorning Master if I did not attend to the queen's daughters."

Again, the queen let it go. "I present to you Eloise Hydra Gumball III and Johanna Umgotteswillen Gumball. Girls, I present you to your Thorning Master."

Together, the twins rose, curtsied, and said, "Welcome, Baroness Thorning, Master to Castle de Brague." They straightened and remained standing.

"I thought they were twins."

"They are, Baroness Thorning Master. Fraternal, not identical."

"Who is firstborn?"

"Eloise," said the queen, pointing. "This one."

The old woman looked from one to the other, cold eyes assessing. "Well, I hope you have raised them with a greater degree of discipline than your mother raised you. Truly, the woman was—" The Thorning Master stopped, thinking the better of it. "Apologies, Queen Eloise. It does not do well for one to speak badly of the deceased." She shook her head. "The old queen, may she stand at Çalaht's side, did the best that she could, I suppose. One can give her that, even if the best she could do was completely inadequate. Mind you, I could have told you that would be the case. Her Thorning Ceremony was just like how she ruled. A mess. Her shortcomings were obvious." She raised her hand so the cane dangled from her palm, and extended her index finger to gesture with quavering jabs in the air. "The Thorning Ceremony tells. The Thorning Ceremony lays bare and reveals. The Thorning Ceremony illuminates. The Thorning Ceremony predicts to those with the eyes to see."

A silence stretched. The Thorning Master's words echoed in Eloise's head long after they'd stopped bouncing around the Receiving Room. She risked a brief sideways glance at Johanna, who looked both appalled and mesmerized.

The Thorning Master rapped her cane down on the marble and shifted her weight back onto it. It was obviously hard for her to stand for so long, but Protocol prevented the queen from offering her a seat, and Eloise doubted Baroness Stúüübenhocker would have accepted it. "So, children, have you made your decision?" She looked from Eloise to Johanna and back, expectant.

Eloise had no idea what she was talking about. "Pardon?"

"What decision?" asked Johanna.

The Thorning Master turned her gaze to the queen. "You did not prepare them?"

"Their preparation is your role, Baroness Thorning Master. I did not want to interfere with your... process."

"My *process* cannot start if they do not assent. Well, fine." She looked again at Eloise. "You have read the *Livre de Protocol*? The section on the Thorning Ceremony?"

"Yes, Baroness Thorning Master," said Eloise.

"And you?"

Johanna nodded.

"I cannot hear that. Try again."

"Yes, Baroness Thorning Master," said Johanna, cheeks reddening.

"And the Commentaries. You've read them?"

"Yes," answered the twins.

"Good. Then let me assure you that you know nothing. Nothing at all. Certainly nothing worthwhile. You might as well know about the sky by someone telling you a little about the color blue. The *Livre* is useless in this matter. Less than useless. It is misleading, both by commission and omission. Here is what you need to know for now, to make your choice: I am the royally appointed Thorning Master. I am tasked with preparing you for the Thorning Ceremony, the most important ritual you will undertake at Court for years, possibly until you are crowned. Your preparation is a task I neither relish nor shirk. It will not be a biscuit walk. If you make it *to* the ceremony, and then if you make it *through* the ceremony, then the words scribbled in those pages might have some relevance. But there is a long, hard, journey between now and when the queen might say anything about your future role in the realm.

"Here is what I demand of you, and this is what you must accept: you will do what I say, as I instruct. I will ask of you what I think is in your best interests, but you must choose to engage. The Thorning Ceremony is not a right or an obligation. It is a privilege. That's one of the many things the *Livre* misses completely. The first step toward that privilege is accepting me as your Thorning Master. If you walk out of this room with me, you do so at your own behest, thereby assenting to these conditions."

Johanna raised her hand to ask a question, her face curious. "And if we do not assent? What then?"

The Thorning Master gave a mirthless laugh. "Nothing, my dear. Nothing. The Thorning Ceremony will come and go and the scribe will record your choice not to undergo it. There have been Gumballs who have made that choice, and others who wish they had. Your mother was not one of the former, but perhaps one of the latter. Your grandmother, the same. Both were under my tutelage. Gumballs have submitted themselves to the Thorning Ceremony back to Agnes Delion Frostbite Gumball, the first Gumball queen, although the ceremony is much older than that. Lesser girls than you have succeeded. Better girls than you have failed. That is the way."

She stopped and looked from one twin to the other. Her expression neither encouraged nor warned them off, but Eloise felt like the Thorning Master could see into her soul. "Follow me, or follow me not. It is your choice, but once made, it cannot be unmade." Then the old woman faced the monarch and nodded. "Queen Eloise. It has been close enough to a pleasure." Without waiting for a response, Baroness Thorning Master Sÿlvia Nûûûttëëërlïïng Stúúùbenhocker née de Gumball turned and began shuffle-shuffle-tock-pausing her way out of the Receiving Room.

Eloise watched her go, thoughts racing. Could she stand to put herself in this ancient woman's control, following whatever whims she had? Eloise felt coerced. She could say no. She could forgo the Thorning Ceremony. But the words in the *Livre* were all about fitness for rule. Her mother had done it. Her grandmother had too, although from what the baroness had said, it had been... inelegant, perhaps? Eloise did not want to sidestep the possibility. And she could not imagine her mother putting this decision in front of her if it were unsafe or damaging. Not permanently so, anyway. How bad could it be? How much could it hurt? But then, why had their mother not spoken to them about it? What was she avoiding, or hiding?

As the old woman reached the threshold of the Receiving Room, Eloise looked at her sister. "Jo?" Johanna was lost in thought. No, that wasn't right. She looked scared. Johanna was blinking back tears and shaking.

Her sister never cried. Ever.

Strangely, that helped Eloise make up her mind. She extended her hand. "Come on, Jo. We can do this."

Johanna looked up, wiped her eyes with the back of her hand and nodded. She laced her fingers into Eloise's and gave a small squeeze. The twins curtsied to their mother, who nodded back, face still carefully blank. Then they turned and walked out of the Receiving Room, putting themselves into the Thorning Master's control.

5

SECLUSION

J ust beyond the threshold, the Thorning Master turned to face them. "I see you have come." Matter-of-fact. Neither surprised nor pleased.

The twins stopped in front of her, keeping a respectful distance. "Yes, Baroness Thorning Master."

"Here is your first instruction. You will do what I say when I say it. If I tell you to eat an orange, you eat the orange. If I say prick your finger, you prick your finger. Some princesses find this harder than others. They are not used to being spoken or dictated to in such a way. See this?" She pointed to the line of thorns in her neck. "You will not have to undergo anything I have not already experienced myself. Understood?"

"Yes, Baroness," said Eloise.

"Yes, ma'am," agreed Johanna.

"Here is your second instruction: you will not speak unless I explicitly give you permission to. Not in my presence, nor away from it. Understood?"

"Yes, Bar—" started Eloise, but the Thorning Master stopped her with a sharp wave of her hand.

"Which part of 'you will not speak' was unclear? That means now. Understood?"

The twins nodded.

"This is my third instruction: you will go to the designated room, where you will be secluded. You will not leave it unless I explicitly give you permission. You will have minimal or no contact with castle and Court, except as directed by me. You will care for yourselves without servants or other interference. You will wear what is provided, study when I dictate, eat only what is given, work as directed, and sleep when I say you may. You will give me your focus, your willingness, your capability. You will spare me your whining, your reluctance, your recalcitrance. I do this for you."

Johanna raised her hand again to ask a question.

"Occasionally, I allow some questions. This is not one of those times. When I do permit questions, I may or may not answer them. Certainly not those I deem frivolous, not germane or, most importantly, where answers reveal too much too soon. Understood?"

They nodded.

"Good. Märgärët!" A pinch-faced servant Eloise had never seen before stepped forward from behind them. She wore the plain, cotton dress and apron of a kitchen maid, but her long, black hair was braided in a knot normally reserved for royalty attending gala events. The incongruity was startling. Eloise guessed she was at most five years older than them. She must have come with the baroness. "Girls, this is Märgärët von den Kleiderschrankbenutzer. All you need to know is that Märgärët's word is my word. Understood?"

Nods.

"Märgärët, escort them to their seclusion."

"Yes, Baroness Thorning Master."

Märgärët led them to a less-used wing of Castle de Brague. Eloise had explored most of the castle, but there were less inviting nooks and any number of disused rooms, and as such, parts of the castle were much less familiar. The servant led them like she'd lived there for years, through corridors, up stairs, and even through a tunnel. Eloise was not lost, exactly, but she was definitely on less familiar ground.

"Here." Märgärët stopped in front of a nondescript door and used a key to open it. She walked into the room ahead of them. It was a little thing, but Eloise noticed. Normally servants let the princesses enter rooms first.

Calling the seclusion room "spare" would have been generous. It was not a prison—it was clean and had windows at the top of the walls without bars across them. There were a few pieces of furniture: two straight-backed wooden chairs, a single table with a slate and chalk, a sideboard, and a pair of cots with unmade straw mattresses folded over. Next to the cots were plain, wooden bedside tables, on each of which sat a neatly folded pile of blankets, sheets, and clothing.

"You are to remain here unless the Baroness or I explicitly give you permission to go elsewhere. If you leave, we will know. If you speak, we will know. Understood?"

The two girls nodded.

"You are to change into those clothes," said Märgärët. "Fold up what you are wearing." She lit an eight-hour candle. "The Baroness will be ready for you in exactly one hour. Between now and then, you may return to your room and select exactly 16 items to have with you here. If you try to bring more, she will know. If you have particular wants while you are in seclusion, you may chalk them onto the slate and I will take your requests to the baroness. If she assents, I will let you know. Understood?"

They nodded again.

"Now get changed," she said, then left the room, closing the door behind her. Eloise half expected to hear the lock click, but it didn't.

Eloise looked around the room. This was going to be a problem. No, that was wrong. The room itself was not a problem. The problem was Eloise—or, more specifically, her particular proclivities. She had habits that needed attending to, habits that helped her navigate from one end of the day to the other—things in their particular places, routines and sequences, objects and mannerisms, all of which provided comfort, relief, or distraction from her tendencies. These practices would not fit into this sparely furnished room, even if modified with 16 of her personal items. Eloise knew what she was like, and worried. She had done her best to hide this from everyone, even Johanna. If she had to attend to her habits in front of her sister, or even avoid doing so, they would become worse. Eloise's mouth dried, and she tried to push the anxiety aside. But sooner rather than later, her habits would demand a reckoning, and she did not know how she'd manage.

Can I have the bed on the right? signed Eloise. It was the one her habits wanted.

Sure. I'm good either way.

Thanks.

Eloise flipped open the straw mattress, sat on the edge of the hard cot, and began unbuttoning her beloved Court day dress. She shimmied out of it, letting it form a puddle on the floor, and picked up the small stack of clothes. The material of both the dress and the undergarments was coarse and unbleached, the same cloth used for maids and servants. It was the first time Eloise had ever put on anything so plain, unrefined, and colorless. The starched stiffness was rough on her skin.

This would take some getting used to.

Johanna had not yet started moving. She shook her head with a pensive, puzzled look, then signed, *What is this supposed to be about?*

Eloise shrugged, *I guess we'll find out.*

Do you trust her?

Which one? asked Eloise. *The baroness or that servant?*

Either.

Neither.

Me either.

Eloise walked over to her sister and gave her shoulder a squeeze. *You going to be OK?*

To be honest, I don't know. I hope so.

Me too.

Eloise pointed at the eight- hour candle and held her thumb and index finger near each other to indicate "small." *We need to hurry if we're going to get our stuff.*

Johanna shook herself, like she was trying to shake off her thoughts. She grabbed her pile of clothes. *Two secs. Be right there.*

✿ 6 ✿

THE SILENCE OF THE JAMS

Minutes later, they were jogging toward their rooms. It would take most of the time they had just to get there and back. As they ran, Eloise thought about how odd it was that they were allowed 16 items. Why 16? Why not 15 or 17 or nine or three? So arbitrary.

The material of her unfamiliar dress swished around her strangely. She felt self-conscious wearing clothes suited to servants. They made her feel like an imposter. What if someone stopped her and asked her to clean or fetch something? If she was supposed to keep silent, how could she explain that wasn't for her to do?

She thought about what she should take back to the seclusion room. Another blanket? A different pillow? Certainly a comb, but then she'd feel the itch to take the other comb and hairbrush that lived with it, even though she didn't need them. Absolutely she'd grab a licorice chew stick for cleaning her teeth. That was two maybes, two definites, and a couple of hangers on. It would be hard to keep to such a small number.

The door to her room was ajar. Stepping inside, she found Läääcy de Aardvark smoothing the last of her dresses back into their trunk. The maid heard her and spun around, losing her grip on the trunk lid, which slammed shut. "Oh!" She curtsied. "I did not expect you so soon. Do you need to be alone? I can leave."

Eloise shook her head.

"I've put all those pretty dresses of yours back in the trunk the way you like them: reds, then oranges, yellows, greens, blues, indigos, and then the violet ones. I did the ribbons that way too. I sometimes have trouble remembering the exact order. Did I get it right?"

Eloise nodded, then shook her head, and pointed to her mouth, meaning she couldn't talk.

"You want me to bring you something else to eat. Right. I cleaned away the remains from earlier. And I promise to do better with the jams. There'll be no need to scold me this time. I'll be firm with Chef, or as firm as I can be. Chef doesn't pay much attention to the likes of me. But quince shall not come close to your scones. Or your toast. Or whatever it is that you're having. What is it that you'd like?"

Eloise shook her head. She pointed to her mouth, then put her vertical index finger across her lips, trying to convey that she couldn't speak.

The aardvark's ears flapped back involuntarily, and she looked like she might be heading toward tears. "I'm sorry, Princess. I'm sorry. I didn't realize I wasn't supposed to talk about the jams again. Forgive me. I promise not to say anything about the jam incident. Mum's the word. The painful embarrassment of the jam matter will not be spoken of again."

Eloise waved her hands to signal that wasn't what she'd meant. She tried again, pointing to herself, then motioning like she was sewing her lips closed, and pointing to herself again.

The aardvark's mouth dropped open, mortified. "You want to have my mouth sewn shut! Oh, Princess, I've offended you so much that you want my mouth sewn shut! Please, Princess. Please don't have that done!" She dropped to her knees and put her head on the floor. Eloise took a step forward, trying to stop her, still making a "no" gesture. But the aardvark could only see her approaching feet, and scuttled backward in fear.

"I know it is in your right to have my lips sewn together, and clearly I've upset you so much that you can't even bring yourself to speak to me. Which I understand. Truly I do. The quince jam disaster is a stain on the honor of my family. I have brought disgrace to my mother and father, and I have ruined your day, bringing you to the point of wordless anger. I promise to do better. Please don't tell Maid I've made such a terrible mistake. She'll deal with me harshly. Maid warned me to tread carefully around you, and she was right. Why can't I learn to listen to what Maid says? I'm stupid and thickheaded and a dolt, and I've caused you unhappiness, and I deserve everything you want to have done to me, but having my mouth sewn shut, even for a little while, would be, would be, would be unspeakable! Oh, Princess, I'm sorry. I'll fix this. Somehow, I'll make this better. You are right to be in your silent rage."

And without warning, she bolted upright, snatched up her rags, duster, broom, and mop, and raced from the room, muttering, "No quince jam, no quince jam, no quince jam" over and over and over.

Eloise watched her go. That was a strange encounter. She considered going after her, but feared she'd only make things worse. Plus, she was running out of time.

The aardvark's behavior left her rattled. What had she said? That Maid had warned her to tread carefully? Whatever for?

Eloise suddenly realized that she didn't have much time left. She snatched up her pillow (did the pillow and pillow case count as separate items?), a blanket, her favorite pair of comfortable shoes (again, was that one item or two?), the licorice chew stick, a bar of lavender and marigold soap, and a change of undergarments. She put everything in the pillow case, then added her comb. Despite her inner urgings, she left its comb and hairbrush neighbors where they sat. She could feel their disappointment.

Eloise still had a few items to pack, but she was feeling rushed and didn't know how long she would be in seclusion. Was it just for today? A week? Forever? She grabbed an apple in case she got hungry, a hockey sack in case she got bored and needed something to toss or kick, and a polished clear quartz she'd found on a walk one day, and that she considered lucky. That left her either three or six more things she could take. She'd call it six, giving herself the benefit of the doubt. A pair of breeks. A tunic. Her favorite necklace. A spare ribbon. And then, somewhat to her embarrassment, she picked up Bo Bo, the stuffed gila monster that was her favorite toy. She'd played and slept with Bo Bo ever since she could remember. Maybe it would help her ignore her habits and be able to fall asleep on that horrible cot and mattress.

She put the gila monster in the pillowcase with everything else, hefted the makeshift bag over her shoulder, took a last look around, then headed back toward the seclusion room.

❧ 7 ❧

TORTURE TOWER

The twins made it back to the seclusion room just as the eight-hour candle burned down to its next mark. Märgärët stood in the doorway, impatient. "There's no time to unpack. Baroness Thorning Master awaits, and we still have to get there. Leave your things on your bed. I will go through them and make sure there is nothing that is not allowed. Hurry!"

Eloise stiffened. The thought of this stranger going through her belongings (and seeing Bo Bo!) made her skin crawl. Nevertheless, she put the pillow case on her bed, and tucked the opening underneath to hide its contents, not that that would make a difference.

Johanna had used a gardening basket for her things, which struck Eloise as much more practical. From what she could see, her sister had chosen similar things of comfort, including her favorite pair of gardening secateurs and Rüüütÿÿÿ, the beloved stuffed toy rutabaga their uncle, King Doncaster, had given her. So Johanna was feeling unsettled, too.

Märgärët motioned for them to follow, and the girls laced hands and fell in behind her. Soon they were walking too fast to comfortably hold hands, so with a little squeeze, Eloise let go.

While the seclusion room was in a disused wing of the castle, the room where the Thorning Master awaited them was in one of the busier spots. Still self-conscious about her dress, Eloise wondered what everyone who saw them would think. Was their training for the Thorning Ceremony a secret? The whispers around Court were usually swift, but the aardvark maid had not seemed to know anything about the cause of her silence. Walking through the main halls of Castle de Brague, wearing the wrong clothes and in enforced silence, Eloise felt inexplicably embarrassed and exposed. She glanced at Johanna whose face was a practiced blank. Just like their mother's when she was trying to pretend that a matter before the throne did not vex her.

When Märgärët reached a spiral staircase, Eloise realized where they were going—a tower on the castle's north side that was officially called North, but had any number of nicknames, including Overlook Tower, Gwendolyn's Folly—as Queen Gwendolyn the Irritable was the one who had it built—and what Eloise and Johanna always called it: the Torture Tower. They called it that because the tower had a single round room at the top with inexplicable iron rings set into its stonework spaced evenly around the circular wall. This suggested to the twins an unsavory history, although there was no actual evidence to support this. Still, the name "Torture Tower" struck their fancy and between them, it stuck.

Märgärët waved them past her. "You'll find the baroness at the top."

The room at the top of the Torture Tower wasn't exactly round—it was more like an octagon, with a glassless window in each side. Eloise loved the spectacular views of Brague and the countryside beyond, although the sheer drop from the windows made her queasy. The room was also drafty and dirty, the roof was prone to leaking in rainy weather, and a few safety rails would not have gone astray. Given the 144 steps up to the top, Eloise was surprised that the Thorning Master chose to meet them there.

In fact, how would she get up there? Had she spent the entire time since they had last seen her hobbling these steps? Had someone carried her? Eloise imagined Baroness Stúüùbenhocker cradled in the arms of one of the more muscled castle guards and immediately wiped the image from her mind. No, that was not the baroness's style.

Did that mean she planned on sleeping in there, or would she make her way up and down those steps every day? Would it be every day? Was this a one-off? Had they hauled a bed up for her?

Eloise did not like not knowing what was going on.

The Thorning Master sat on a high stool behind a table, her back to the spectacular vista. She frowned when the twins entered the room, then glared from one to the other. "I expect punctuality. No, more than that. I expect you to anticipate. To be early. You will never leave me waiting again. When we are to meet, you will arrive early, and you will leave when I say, 'Dismissed.'"

They nodded.

Eloise glanced around. There were no other stools. Were they supposed to stand for the whole time? And if so, how long would that be?

"You," the baroness said, pointing to Johanna. "Go to that wall. And you, go to the one that's two sections along. Look at the ring on the wall opposite you. You may choose to sit, or not."

Eloise walked to her spot, placed herself exactly between the two edges of the octagon section, and looked at the iron ring opposite.

She waited for something to happen. The Thorning Master was obviously comfortable with silences. She allowed one to sit for a very long time. Eloise found her mind wandering. Her eyes drifted off the iron torture ring and out the window. The weather was nice, but it looked like a storm might be gathering. She could hear the call of "Rice! Rice!" from Old Man Wälker, the rice monger, down in the markets. Eloise particularly liked his jasmine rice. What did standing here have to do with the ceremony? And how long was this preparation going to take? Would they get lunch?

Out of nowhere, a bamboo switch snapped Eloise on the shoulder. The sting of it shocked her, and she rounded on the Thorning Master, who still sat on her high stool, a long bamboo stalk held in her right hand. "How dare you!"

"How dare I?" The baroness laughed. A genuine, deep laugh. "How dare I?" She stood up and hobbled over so she was just weak lengths away from Eloise. "Discipline. You lack discipline. I gave you a simple task. Stand and look at a single spot. Apparently this is beyond your capabilities. Both of you failed. Miserably. Try again. Your task is to look at the ring. And to remain silent. You failed at that as well."

Eloise was not used to being spoken to this way. Her mother and father might do it, maybe, but no one else.

She chose not to reply.

There must be something important about the iron ring, some significance. Eloise brought her attention to it, considering its shape, color, texture, and size. It struck her as distinctly uninteresting. Her nose itched, and she reached up a hand to scratch it.

This time, she heard the bamboo switch right before it popped her. "Be still," commanded the baroness.

This was going to get old fast.

Eloise risked sitting down on the stone floor, crossing her legs. She guessed that leaning against the wall might earn another swat—the Thorning Master struck her as a no-leaning-against-the-wall kind of person—so she made herself as comfortable as possible, straightened her back, and started looking at the stupid ring again.

Another thwack. Eloise flinched, but this time it was Johanna. "Wake up," said Stúúùbenhocker. "Focus."

And so it went for what felt like a decade, but from the movement of the sun, was probably only two or three hours. Johanna eventually sat as well, and the two of them did their best to look at their respective rings, sit straight, not let their thoughts wander, and endure what Eloise was certain was the dullest afternoon of her life—even worse than the worst of Master Overbolt's Protocols and Procedures lessons.

Eventually, the Thorning Master hefted herself from her stool. She put down the bamboo rod on the table and balanced on her cane. "Stand."

Eloise teetered upward on legs that had fallen asleep and did her best to ignore the pins and needles that rushed in. She had to grab the window sill to steady herself.

"You have made a calamitously bad start today. I suggest strongly that you practice this exercise on your own. Get better at it. Is that a simple enough direction for you to understand?"

They nodded.

"You will wait while I descend."

Without another word, she turned to the stairs. Eloise and Johanna listened as Baroness Stúüübenhocker shuffled down the steps, slowly, methodically, without a break. It was obvious from the inadvertent grunts and the occasional muttered oath that every step hurt her.

As was Eloise's habit, she counted each painful step of the Thorning Master's journey downward. By step 20, she was breathing as hard as a 20-strong-length runner. Around step 100, the sounds of discomfort grew more faint, but were most certainly there. Eloise guessed at the passage of steps based on how long the previous one took.

Between the piercings she wore and the determined, painful steps she took, one thing was abundantly clear: by Çalaht's whistling nose hairs, Baroness Sÿlvia Nûûûttëëërlïïïng Stúüübenhocker née de Gumball was one tough biscuit.

Eventually, a single word echoed up the staircase, clear and sharp.

"Dismissed."

❧ 8 ❧

APPARENTLY NOT VALUED

Märgärët stood, arms folded, waiting for them when they reached the bottom of the stairs. "You will walk with me back to the seclusion room."

So, no ducking away. (It occurred to Eloise that she should wonder what ducks thought of that phrase. She'd have to ask one sometime, when she was allowed to speak again.)

Back they walked, passing a cluster of maids carrying linens. They paused in surprise at seeing the twins, leaned in to each other, whispered, snickered, and glanced back at the princesses. Eloise felt a mix of anger and embarrassment flush her cheeks. Anger she was used to. Embarrassment, too. But the two together? Less familiar. If she had been allowed to speak, her anger probably would have won, but being silenced meant that embarrassment dominated.

At the far side of the castle, Märgärët once again went through the door first. Again, it rankled. Plus, somehow, in Eloise's head, the room had gone from the seclusion room to the Seclusion Room. She wasn't sure this was a good thing.

"You will unpack," said Märgärët. "That which is valued, you will find a place for. You will be here a while. You should find your place here, too."

Great. Just great.

The servant knelt at the fireplace, picked up the flint and steel, and began sparking the already-set pile of leaves and twigs.

Eloise's pillow case was where she had left it, but the things in it had been moved. She picked up Bo Bo and set the toy gila monster next to her pillow, then sorted through the other items. Everything was still there, except for the apple. Eloise felt an inexplicable pang of loss, and a much more understandable flash of annoyance.

A guttural noise ripped from the other side of the room. Johanna slammed her basket down on the table, snatched up the slate and chalk, scratched something furious, and held it up for Märgärët.

The servant ignored her, focused on gently puffing a nascent flame.

Johanna tapped the slate with the chalk to get her attention.

Märgärët continued to encourage the fire, adding larger and larger twigs. When there was a decent blaze, the servant straightened, wiped her hands on her apron and looked at Johanna, who continued to seethe. She glanced at the slate. "I can't read your writing."

Johanna, barely containing her rage, wiped the slate with her sleeve and scratched new lines. Moments later, she flipped the slate around for Märgärët. Eloise walked to where she could see what was on it as well. She'd drawn a pair of secateurs and a question mark.

Märgärët clasped her hands in front of her. "I have taken them."

Johanna rapped the slate again, and mouthed, "Why?"

"Items that you might possibly use to do harm to yourself are strictly forbidden. No food, and nothing you could use for injury."

Johanna was livid, and Eloise knew why. Her sister had those pruning shears with her all the time. Her garden was her sanctuary, her plants her friends and confidants. The servant may as well have taken a couple of her fingers. Johanna stuck out her palm, jabbing it toward the servant. Her meaning was clear: "Give them back."

"No," said Märgärët. "No."

Johanna jabbed again, eyes fierce.

Märgärët stared at her, unruffled. "I have made myself abundantly clear. However, perhaps additional explanation is required. When you walked out of the Receiving Room and followed the Thorning Master, you agreed to put yourself into her care and command. She told you that I speak for her, and I do. Consider these her words. While you are under her care and command, you will do what she tells you, and you will follow her rules. Silence is one of them. Eating that which is provided is a second. Not having potentially dangerous items on your person is another. Making the effort to care for the things that you value is a fourth. For example, that." She pointed at Eloise's Court dress on the floor. "Is that an item that you value?"

Eloise nodded.

"One could not tell by looking. Pick it up and fold it neatly."

Eloise opened her mouth to say something, but managed to hold her tongue. Who was this girl to tell her what to do? Eloise would pick it up or not, as suited her. She would certainly not be taking direction from a servant she had not known two days before.

"I said, pick it up and fold it. Neatly."

Maybe it was the hours of staring stupidly at the iron ring. Maybe it was sympathetic ire over Johanna's stolen pruning shears. Maybe it was simply being spoken to as if she did not matter, or have any say. But Eloise refused. Flat out, no way, absolutely not. It was her dress, she would do as she pleased with it.

Märgärët looked at her with an expression that vaguely reminded Eloise of her mother. The servant had certainly not earned *that* right.

"One more time. Pick it up and fold it."

Eloise, arms folded, did not move. She shook her head.

"This is your last warning."

Eloise stayed still.

"Very well then." Märgärët walked over to the aquamarine Court day dress and picked it up by the shoulders, holding it so she could see all of it. Her manner changed to admiration. She scrutinized the front and then turned it so she could see the back. "Truly beautiful," she whispered, running a finger along the stitching. "Such an even, perfect line of stitches on the hem. And the embroidering. My mother used to do this kind of needlework. A rose in half-blossom like this? Days and days could go into it." She petted the dress like it was a precious connection to family. And maybe it was. Had her mother been the one to sew it?

Then with incredible care and delicacy, she laid it on the bed and folded it to perfection, sleeves tucked, hems aligned, edges perfectly squared. A neat bundle ready for storage. "There. That's what I meant. Not so hard, really."

Then she picked up the dress, walked to the fireplace, and threw it into the flames. It ignited immediately.

Eloise was gobsmacked. "My dress! How dare you—"

"Silence!" She slashed a hand through the air like she could cut through the sound itself.

The crackle and smell of burning cloth wafted into the room. This servant girl was out of control.

Except, she wasn't. The act was cold, deliberate. She was completely in control. She did not radiate anger, hatred, or violence. At most, she seemed disappointed. "Such a waste," Märgärët said. "But apparently you did not value it enough to give it care. Perhaps now you will."

Without another word, she left the room.

This time, the lock clicked behind her.

❦ 9 ❦

DRAPING SHEETS

Dawn snuck its way into the Seclusion Room, and Eloise saw that Johanna was also already awake.

G'morning, signed Eloise.

G'morning. You OK?

Why?

Sounded to me like you didn't sleep much either, signed Johanna.

Nope. Not used to this. Hate it.

Eloise watched Johanna wipe her eyes. So she wasn't the only one in silent tears. They sat up on the uncomfortable beds.

I can't believe she took my secateurs, or what she did to your dress.

She's an [indistinct gesture].

Agreed.

Eloise smoothed the blanket across her knee. *How am I going to get through this?*

You *aren't going to get through this.* We *are going to get through this.*

Thanks. That helps.

The door lock clanked, the girls dropped their hands to their laps, and the [indistinct gesture] came in. "Get dressed, eat something, and be ready to come with me in ten minutes," said Märgärët.

Eloise had never been a morning person, and her feelings about this particular morning were no different. Her morning routine usually consisted of trying to wait it out, but clearly that was not an option with Märgärët, so she shoved off the blanket, took a sip of water, began chewing her licorice tooth twig to clear her breath, and swapped night clothes for the previous day's servant outfit, which had not folded itself, cleaned itself, or hung itself out to air overnight. Eloise couldn't remember the last time she wore the same garment two days in a row. When she was four, she had a single favorite dress, and had insisted on wearing it for a month. But not since then.

She was just tying on her slippers when Märgärët returned. She handed each twin a pair of sturdy, brownish clod-hoppers and a pair of thick socks. "Wear these."

The shoes were chunky, graceless, and familiar to her as standard issue for the servant girls. Märgärët wore a similar pair, though hers looked better quality and were a deep black, instead of dun brown like the ones she'd given them. The socks were as thick as three pairs of her normal stockings. Were they going on a hike? A trek to the other side of the realm? What possible reason could there be to put on such ghastly footwear?

Eloise untied her slippers and pulled on the socks. *Of course, they're scratchy*, she thought. The heavy shoes looked like they were 20 sizes too large, but they actually fit when pulled over the socks. It reminded her of being a child, playing dress-ups and clunking around in her father's boots.

"Come, we do not want to be late."

Märgärët led them through the castle halls, past the kitchen, and out into a shed.

The laundry shed.

What could Märgärët possibly want them to do here?

They found the shed in full swing, even though the sun was not yet fully above the horizon. The smell of lavender-scented olive soap hung thick. Eloise recognized it as the smell of her bed sheets, if fainter. A dozen servant boys and girls paddled cauldrons, rubbed clothes against washboards, and piled wet linens into baskets. They all stopped and stared, gape-mouthed, at the twins, until the matron in charge, a hippopotamus in a lead servant's cap and apron, quietly cleared her throat. At that small sound, they launched back into their labors, not giving the twins a second glance.

Märgärët led them to the hippo. "This morning you will help the Court Laundress, Íïïtáää Kréëëpläääch. Have you met Mistress Kréëëpláääch before?"

Eloise and Johanna both shook their heads.

"Don't you know to curtsy?" asked Märgärët. "I thought you knew your Protocol."

Eloise felt certain Protocol would say that the Court Laundress should curtsy to them. Apparently not. She and Johanna both curtsied to the hippo, who acknowledged them with a small nod. Like she was queen, thought Eloise. What, was she queen of the laundry?

"Mistress Kréëëpláääch will give you your tasks and make sure you execute them to Court standards. Is this clear?"

Eloise raised her hand, but since there was no slate, drew "Why?" one letter at a time on her palm where Märgärët could see it.

Märgärët looked at her like she was simple. "Perhaps you can figure that out while you work. Do as Mistress Kréëëpláääch directs. She and the others know you cannot speak. I will collect you when it is time for you to see the baroness."

Eloise had certainly seen Íïtáää Kréëëplääàch around the castle—not many hippos cared for the variable climate found at Brague. She even knew Kréëëplääàch had something to do with the laundry, but didn't realize she was in charge. Perhaps becoming Court Laundress was recent. Eloise didn't follow those sorts of things.

"Children, let's start you with something easy," the hippo said. Her voice had a surprising lilt, and her tone was kind. Kréëëplääàch led them to where sturdy reed baskets filled with sheets sat on low racks dripping into drains. A girl their age picked a basket up by the handles, then set it down as the hippo approached, and bowed—to the hippo, not the twins. "This is Gerta. Gerta, be a dear and show our new helpers how to drape the sheets."

"Yes, ma'am. Please grab a basket, Prin—"

The hippo cleared her throat, interrupting.

"Sorry, ma'am. Please, uh, you and you, if you would be so kind as to grab a basket each."

Eloise picked one off the drip rack. It felt like it weighed two strong weights, although realistically she knew it was probably more like seven or ten weights. Wetness from the sheets leaked through the reeds into her skirts. Delightful. She and Johanna struggled to lug their baskets behind Gerta, who seemed to have no problems carrying hers. Eloise wondered if it was lighter.

Gerta led them to a huge sunny courtyard filled with row after row of a single kind of bush, washerwoman's boxwood, planted like a crop. Someone had made a big effort to trim them to a standard low, arch-shaped continuous hedge—the world's most boring topiary. Interspersed with the boxwoods were lavender plants, giving the courtyard the smell of perfume.

Draping the sheets meant just that—laying them over bushes so they could dry in the sun. Eloise and Johanna went to different rows and, following Gerta's lead, set their baskets on the ground.

"You and you, if I may show you how the draping is done, thusly." Gerta took two corners of a wet sheet and flung it like she might be covering a bed. The sheet spread out and lay perfectly positioned on the shrubbery—one efficient motion that was the result of years of practice. Gerta tugged it a little to position it closer to the previous sheet, and then she was done, ready for the next one.

Eloise tried to imitate her, but her throw produced a wet pile of tangled sheet that she then had to untwist and peel apart. She tried again with the next sheet, and again with the next. Not only did it take Eloise three times as long as Gerta to lay out a sheet, but by the time her basket was empty, her dress was soaked through.

Doing laundry was stupid.

Gerta had spent the extra time retrieving and folding dry sheets. She came back with an armload and shook her head. "I'm sorry, Prin— I mean, I'm sorry, you and you. But your sheets are not laying correctly. Mistress Kréëèplää̈äch is quite particular about these things."

"Indeed, I am." The hippo emerged into the courtyard, and Gerta immediately dropped into as much of a curtsy as she could while holding a stack of linens. Eloise did not, and Johanna split the difference with an awkward half bow. "That's fine, Gerta. Perhaps you could get your next basket while I chat with our new helpers."

Gerta scurried off, and the Court Laundress walked over to Eloise's sheets. She gave them a quick look over, then did the same for Johanna's. "Well, I guess we can't expect too much too soon. Let me give you some feedback."

The feedback covered the distance between the sheets, their straightness, their orientation on the bushes, how parallel they were to the ground, and the number of allowable creases (none). She had Eloise and Johanna adjust each sheet until they were positioned creaseless and perfect, then went into the differences between sheets for varying mattress sizes, what to do if one happens to find a stain, what to do if one finds a tear, how to remove a sheet from the bushes, how to fold the sheet into exact proportions and with the seams aligned, how to stack the folded sheets so the seams all faced the same way with the seamless folds all lined up on one side, and how to use pronged fasteners to attach the sheets to the bushes if it was windy.

Eloise had no idea that laundry was so complicated. And this was just hanging it out and collecting it.

They followed the hippo back to the laundry room. All the servants bowed when she entered. There were more baskets on the drip racks than when they'd left. Dozens more, with more on the way, from the look of it. "If you could please hang out the rest of the laundry, that would be lovely. If you have any questions, Gerta will be happy to answer them if you can convey them in silence."

"Yes," agreed Gerta, who was grabbing her next basket. "You and you can silently ask me anything you and you need."

Eloise forced a grin, nodded thanks to Gerta, bowed the tiniest of bows to Mistress Kréëëpláääch, grasped the handles of her next basket, and heaved it off the rack. This one was definitely heavier and wetter than the first.

She and Johanna spent the next several hours lugging heavy, sheet-filled baskets to the drying yard, draping the sheets on the hedges, positioning them, positioning them again until they were perfect, folding dry sheets, and returning them to the shed. Eloise took some satisfaction in the fact that her sheet throwing got better with practice, although she soon realized that meant she was more productive, which meant more of her time was spent schlepping the wet loads.

The only words anyone spoke to them came from Kréëëpláääch, who said, "Faster, please," over and over, if politely, until Eloise felt like she was running from the drying rack to the washerwoman boxwoods and back.

It was the hardest Eloise had ever worked in her life. She couldn't imagine doing this every day, and sincerely hoped the morning's work was a one-off.

By the time Märgärët came and got them, the sun was high overhead, they had moved from sheets and bedding to towels and washcloths, and all Eloise wanted to do was get out of her wet clothes and have a nap.

No such luck. Despite her sodden dress and her exhaustion, it was time for their next lesson. Eloise just hoped she'd be able to stay awake.

❧ 10 ❧

SQUEAMISH

The orange mocked her. The orange and the healing needles, both. Eloise felt them laughing at her and her inability to skewer the former with the latter.

Days and days had passed since the baroness had taken over their lives. Almost a week of no talking, the same starched, drab, scratchy clothes, servants and maids pointing at her like she was a source of amusement, arduous, monotonous manual labor in the laundry, at the blacksmith's, at the ditcher's, with the sappers, or in the Bureau of Bladed Weapons. All that was followed by the incessant attempts to focus like an idiot on the torture rings in the tower.

At least the orange and needle mockery provided distraction from all that.

Eloise decided it was possible she imagined their sniggering. There had not been a lot of food, certainly, much less than she was used to. The Thorning Master seemed to think thin miso soup was adequate sustenance. Eloise begged to differ.

Sticking the healing needles into the citrus was supposed to simulate the resistance and feel of a needle going into human skin. She guessed it was to give them a sense of what would happen to her and Johanna. Maybe she was hungry and fatigued, but she genuinely had trouble doing it. Too much empathy for the orange. Too many memories of the healing needles going into her own skin to cure aches and pains.

Johanna did not have such a debilitating empathy with her fruit. Hers looked like an echidna.

"Problem?" The Thorning Master hovered above Eloise.

Eloise shook her head. She'd started thinking of Baroness Stúüübenhocker as "Old Pincushion," and in a way was glad she could not speak, as she might have slipped up and said it out loud.

"Then finish the task. Trust me, there will be plenty of other chances to be squeamish."

Eloise nodded and shoved a needle into the orange. Its skin resisted just a little, then yielded to the point. "Sorry," she thought as she impaled the orange seven more times. "But better you than me."

Baroness Stúüübenhocker shuffled back to her stool. She placed both palms on the table, steadying herself. "Despite your slow progress and lack of discipline, we need to continue," she said. "There are things you must learn. The *Livre de Protocol* and Commentaries are woefully inadequate when describing the Thorning Ceremony, so it is up to me to make sure you are ready. Understood?"

The twins both nodded.

"Then let us begin that part of your learning. Märgärët!"

The servant girl appeared in the doorway. "Yes, Baroness?"

"I am speaking of the Thorning Ceremony now. You will attend my words."

"Yes, Baroness." She walked into the room and without being told, took a spot two octagon panels along to Johanna's left. She remained standing. Eloise had given her as little mind as she could ever since the incident with the Court dress. She obeyed where she had to, but gave nothing else.

"There are 16 thorns involved in the Thorning Ceremony. Each comes from a different kind of plant, representing various regions of the realms. Each has a name, its own symbolism, and is placed into a different part of the body, thus adding to the symbolism. As you will eventually learn, if you are capable of it, there is some degree of choice in the ceremony. How you choose reflects who you are. I suggest you choose well, although from what I've seen, I do not have a lot of hope. The thorns differ greatly in length, girth, and sharpness. Most affect the body when placed in the skin, but the effects also differ. I will cover all of this. I will teach you everything you need to know. But you must be capable of learning it, absorbing it, and following direction. Neither of you has proven particularly adept. I look forward to being pleasantly surprised on that account."

She let the silence linger. Eloise had learned that this kind of verbal disparagement tended to precede revelations or information, often unpleasant. She could hardly wait for what would come next.

The Thorning Master slid open a drawer in the table, which Eloise had not noticed was there. She removed three small hemp parchment scrolls, a roll of cotton, and a narrow, stoppered vial. She uncorked the vial, removed four needles from a liquid that smelled like it had some sort of alcohol in it, and placed them on the spread cotton. The needles looked ten weak lengths long and were red for a weak length back from the point.

Eloise began to feel a bit woozy.

"There is one thing you need to know about the Thorning Ceremony, which is not documented in any of the writings you've seen, but which is part of the ceremony's tradition dating back centuries. It is this: you place the thorns yourself. It is up to you to master yourself enough to pierce your own flesh with the different thorns during the ritual. If you make it through the ceremony, then you will be assigned a handmaid who will remove the thorns and apply the Wisdom Salve. But the placement of the thorns, the piercing of the skin—this is up to you."

Eloise became more light-headed with every word.

"That part of your training starts now. Come forward."

The baroness motioned, and the twins stood and walked to the table. Märgärët did the same, like she was an equal in this.

"These healing needles are thinner and sharper than most of the thorns you will use. They are a good place to start. Observe."

The Thorning Master picked up one of the needles from the cotton, splayed her left hand flat against the table, and deftly jabbed the healing needle into the fleshy part of her hand between her thumb and forefinger, sinking it so that the weak length of red no longer showed.

Eloise's world went unexpectedly dark, and she slumped to the ground, narrowly avoiding smacking her head on the table as she fell.

❧ II ❧
FAINTER

"**B**y Çalaht's gangrenous goiter, she's a fainter," muttered Stúúùbenhocker. "That would be about right. Märgärët, my box."

"Yes, Baroness." The servant ducked out of the room and returned moments later carrying a wooden box by a handle. She placed it on the table in front of the Thorning Master.

The old woman released a latch, opened the lid, and retrieved another stoppered vial. "Use this," she said, handing it to Märgärët.

"Yes, Baroness." The servant leaned down over Eloise's body, uncorked the vial, and wafted it under the girl's nose.

Eloise gasped awake, jerked upward, hit her head on the table leg, and slumped back down. Märgärët slid her to a safer spot, administered another whiff, and again, Eloise jerked to alertness. This time, she remained sitting upright, shaking her head to clear it of its fog and the smell of sal ammoniac mixed with lavender and eucalyptus. "What happened?" she croaked, then realized who she was with and clasped a hand over her mouth.

The baroness gave her a disappointed head shake, but spared her a rebuke. "Remain kneeling and hold on to the table. You need to see." She held up her hand to show the needle still protruding. "This is what I want you to do. I suggest you use the method that I demonstrated." She removed the needle, then repeated the process of skewering herself in the hand. "Palm flat, fingers wide, and in. Make sure it is deep enough that no red can be seen."

Next, she held up one of the scrolls. "This is your incentive. It contains the details of what you need to memorize. If you succeed in this simple, not very painful task, I will give you the scroll. If you fail, then you must learn through my spoken words." She waggled the scroll. "Having this will make your life much simpler between now and when the ceremony takes place. Now, take a needle and proceed."

Märgärët moved first. She took a needle, spread out her hand, and jabbed herself as if she had done so a hundred times before. Perhaps she had, thought Eloise, gripping the table and fighting back another bout of fainting.

The baroness nodded and handed her servant a scroll.

"Thank you, Baroness," said Märgärët. She pulled the needle out, put it back into the vial with the liquid, and went back to her spot by the wall.

Stúüùbenhocker looked from one twin to the other, waiting.

Johanna went next. She followed the servant's lead by picking up a needle and jabbing her hand swiftly, without time for thought. Eloise saw her sister wince, gasp, and tear up, but she controlled herself. She even held up her hand, so the Thorning Master could see the needle sticking out of it, no red visible.

The old woman nodded and gave Johanna a scroll. She pulled out the needle—Eloise saw the skin tent a bit before it came free—and put it back into the vial with the others.

That left Eloise with all six eyes upon her.

She hate, hate, hated the idea of poking the needle into herself. Eloise had one extremely deep memory of needles. They were five years old, and Seamstress Linttrap had the unenviable task of instructing the girls in the fine art of sewing. They were supposed to sew a simple bag to hold a wooden flute from two rectangles of felt. Seamstress Linttrap, not the most patient of echidnas, got them to thread needles, tie a small knot in the end, and then begin stitching together the thick pieces of cloth. She insisted on perfection and gave constant feedback about stitch tightness and spacing. Eloise hadn't minded it for the first and second sides of the project. It took some doing to get the needles through the tough felt, but she could see her flute case taking shape.

Two stitches into the third side, Eloise got distracted as she shoved on the needle, and glanced away. Her thumb was on the other side, and the sharp sewing needle went in one side and out the other, skewering her like a veggie kebab.

They told her later that her screams were heard across the castle, as far as the Flinging Field. She couldn't imagine how that would even be possible, but the yelling must have been impressive.

Needles, whether healing or sewing, had been a thing ever since.

Eloise picked up a needle, fumbled it, and watched it plink to the floor. She reached to pick it up but the Thorning Master stopped her. "Use a fresh one. But if you ruin that one, your chance for today is over. As is your chance for the scroll. Understood?"

Eloise nodded, and very carefully picked up another needle from the cotton. Holy Çalaht, it looked like it would hurt. She pictured splaying her hand, feeling the cold of the table. She imagined shoving the needle in. In her mind she experienced the sharp pain shooting through her hand, her vain attempts to stifle her screams and tears.

Black flecks of nothingness dotted her vision. Her head felt light.

The bamboo switch whipped the table in front of Eloise. The shock of the "crack" brought her back to awareness. She was in the Torture Tower. She was not lying on the floor. She had not smelled the awful vial. She had not fully fainted. Well, that was something.

"If you insist on fainting every time I ask you to do something, it will make for a dull, tedious process." The baroness's sharp voice cut through any residual muzziness in Eloise's mind. The Thorning Master slapped down the switch again for emphasis. "Less thinking. More doing. Now."

Eloise nodded again and spread her palm flat. Old Pincushion had done it. Märgärët had done it. Even Johanna had done it. Eloise's breathing got faster, moving dangerously toward hyperventilation. *This is going to hurt*, she told herself. *This is really going to hurt. Just like the wood flute bag sewing incident.* Eloise knew it was the wrong self-talk, but it was all she had.

"Do it!" snapped the baroness. "I said do it or the scroll is lost to you. Do it I say! Do it now!"

Tears streamed. Eloise tried to blink them away, and when that didn't work, she wiped them with the back of the hand holding the needle. *Just jab it in*, she thought.

The Thorning Master was suddenly at her side. She gripped Eloise's left wrist, anchoring it to the table with surprising strength. "Do it, child. Stop sniveling and do it. Now. Now!"

Eloise shook her head no.

"You will."

"No."

"Silence!"

Eloise could barely see her hand through her tears. She cried openly, hot, ashamed tears.

"For the love of Çalaht," said the old woman, disgusted. "Have you never been treated with healing needles?" The Thorning Master, still holding Eloise's left hand fast to the table, gripped her right hand, pinching the needle firmly in place. "Look me in the eyes, child. Focus on my eyes."

Eloise did as commanded. She met and held the old woman's gaze.

"Do you give me permission to help you?"

It was the last thing Eloise expected to hear. Was this a trick? She hesitated, then nodded assent.

Keeping her eyes locked on Eloise's, the Thorning Master's voice was firm and cold. "I am going to guide your right hand and help you place the needle into your left hand. I have done this for many years. I know how to do this. I cannot promise that you won't feel it or that it won't hurt. I can guarantee that the discomfort will not be as great as you fear. You have made a monster in your head, but that is the only place the monster resides. You must get past this, or you will fail. Do you understand? Do you give me permission to do what must be done?"

Eloise wanted to scream "no!", snatch away her hand, and run—out of the tower, through the halls and into her room with her nice clothes, her things just the way she liked them. But she didn't. Keeping her eyes on the old woman's, with great trepidation, Eloise slowly, deliberately nodded agreement.

The Thorning Master turned to her servant. "You saw her agree?"

"Yes, Baroness," said Märgärët.

"You?" she asked Johanna. Eloise's sister nodded.

"Good." The Thorning Master still held Eloise's hands, the left one splayed and flat, the right one pinching the needle. Her eyes came back to Eloise's, and it looked like the tiniest of smiles crinkled the side of her mouth. To Eloise's surprise the baroness relaxed. Her shoulders drooped, her hands, still holding Eloise's, loosened their grip slightly, but her eyes remained fixed, mesmerizing. Eloise thought Old Pincushion might actually let go. She, too, relaxed. Maybe there was more instruction that would help Eloise achieve this odious task. Explanation, rationale, and citations of Protocol describing why all this was necessary.

The Thorning Master moved like a mongoose, never breaking eye contact. Before Eloise could figure out what was happening, the baroness gripped her right hand more firmly again, and with a deft, almost bored motion, thrust it downward.

The needle jabbed into the flesh between thumb and index finger, perfectly equidistant between the two. Its red tip was hidden by Eloise's layers of skin.

"Do not move," whispered the Thorning Master, still holding Eloise's left hand, but gripping Eloise's chin with her other. "And do not faint."

Eloise willed herself to stay conscious, choking back the screams she could hear in her head. *It hurts!*

It hurt. But she realized it was tolerable. Her hand stung, but not as much as she would have guessed. Eloise's breathing raced, but she managed to stay present.

The old woman let go and shuffled back to her stool. She sat and folded her arms, looking at Eloise. "It is one of the points the healers use. If you do it right, you could do it all day. Now pull it out."

Eloise did not hesitate. There was no way she'd leave it in there. She gripped the end of the needle between thumb and forefinger and yanked it free.

Eloise placed the needle in the vial, happy to be rid of it. If she thought the Thorning Master might acknowledge the small success, she was mistaken. "No scroll for you," said the baroness. "That was pathetic. Do you think I will do that at the Thorning Ceremony for you as well?"

Eloise felt mortification flood her cheeks. She shook her head meekly.

The old woman slid off her seat and grabbed her cane. She moved to hobble down the stairs. "Märgärët!"

"Yes, Baroness?"

"Make sure that her hand is clean, and any wound treated."

"Yes, Baroness."

"You." The old woman pointed her cane at Johanna. "Keep your scroll to yourself. Do not show her."

Johanna nodded.

Turning to Eloise, she added, "And don't you look at it." Then the Thorning Master was gone, leaving Eloise cradling her hand in her lap, embarrassed.

✥ 12 ✥

JEROME

Eloise sat on the edge of her cot holding her lightly bandaged left hand. She didn't like being too introspective, as that meant confronting all kinds of unpleasant thoughts, but there was no escaping what was going on: she was feeling sorry for herself. Very sorry. It was not how she liked feeling, but there it was.

Not even the haggleberry tea that Märgärët brought her had shifted her mood. It was lukewarm and didn't have any of Chef's nice biscuits with it. The mediocre tea encapsulated just how unpleasant this whole thing was turning out to be.

How would she ever get through this stupid Thorning Ceremony? The longer this went, the stupider she thought the whole thing was.

Johanna sat cross-legged on her cot, but hers was a totally different mood. She'd waited until Märgärët had left them, then carefully unscrolled her reward. She'd spent the last half hour staring at it, while Eloise staring at her, trying to glean what she could from her changing expression. Mostly it looked like disgust, mixed with disbelief.

Normally, Eloise would have just walked over, sat down next to her sister, and had a look. But Baroness Stúüùbenhocker had her spooked.

She had brought her own servant, so it was just as easy for her to bring a fly, bird, or gecko to keep an eye on what went on in the Seclusion Room.

Eloise waved to get her sister's attention. *How bad is it?* she signed.

Bad.

How bad?

Bad.

Can you tell me anything at all?

Probably shouldn't. You never know who's watching or listening.

Eloise shrugged in agreement. Clearly, Johanna was thinking along the same lines as her.

Going to check my garden.

You shouldn't. We're not allowed to go out.

Don't care. Not willing to lose any plants. Plus, I need some quiet.

Eloise did not point out the obvious fact that they were as quiet as they had ever been in their lives. She understood that Johanna needed to get her thoughts in order, but what had she seen in the scroll that prompted that need?

Johanna tucked her scroll under her pillow, picked up her gardening basket (sans pruning shears), opened the door, and was gone.

Very bold, thought Eloise. Maybe she should also break the "Don't go anywhere" rule and head out for a run. For years, Eloise had run around in the castle, but only in the way of children. Recently she'd taken to running as a thing to do for itself. She liked the way it made her feel, and it was one way to give her habits something to do that did not make her look weird. Her mother told her running was unladylike, but her father said it did no harm, and encouraged her to continue, so she did.

She was still debating whether to go out without leave, when there was a tap-tap, tap-tap, tap-tap at the window. She looked up. What sort of person would sit high on a castle ledge and knock? She ignored it.

The sound came again. Tap-tap, tap-tap, tap-tap. Then, "El? Elroy, are you in there?"

Eloise could not help smiling.

Jerome Abernatheen de Chipmunk was her best friend (who was not her twin). He was the son of the Court Seer, Maybelle de Chipmunk, which gave him the right to a Court education. Over the past few years, as they shared classes and tutors, Eloise had grown fond of the nervous, quick-witted, bushy tailed, flamboyantly dressed rodent.

Eloise dragged the table over to the wall, stood on it, and stretched as high as she could. Her fingers just reached the window latch. She unlocked it, but the window had clearly not been opened in forever. With the two of them tugging and shoving, they finally pried it open a few weak lengths—enough for a chipmunk to get through.

Jerome squeezed through the crack, snagging, but not tearing, his pantaloons, which were a shade of orange that screamed "what are you doing wearing us with a pink tunic?" He brushed himself off, reached back outside, hauled in a bag from the window ledge , and handed it to her. Jerome then stepped down onto Eloise's hand, and she lowered him to the table. The chipmunk looked at her face, then at her clothes, then the bandage on her hand. "In the name of Çalaht's braided back hair, I've been looking for you everywhere."

Eloise gave him a hug. She didn't care if anyone was watching. It was good to see him. She picked up the slate and wrote. *Can't talk. Sorry.*

"Yeah, I heard about that. Are you really going to have a bunch of thorns shoved into you? That's got to be the stupidest ritual I've ever heard of. 'Hey everyone, look at me! I'm a porcupine!' Awful."

That's rude to porcupines, she wrote. *And such is Protocol.*

"I know, I know. 'Protocol.' But it's not like the *Livre de Protocol* is the *Scrolls of Çalaht*, where every word and dot of punctuation is supposed to be holy. Controversial, but holy. It's Protocol. There are commentaries. Opinions. Surely someone is of the opinion that you don't have to stick a bunch of thorns into yourself just because you're in line for the throne?"

You've been reading up!

"Just call me Mr. Curiosity."

Good to see you. Horrible here.

"What happened to your hand?"

Eloise mimed placing her hand on the table, holding a needle in her other hand, and then poking one into the other. Her mime may have exaggerated the force involved.

"You're kidding."

Not kidding.

He pointed at the bag he'd brought. "That's for you. Happy not-birthday."

It was food. Three figs, some strips of peach leather, a handful of cashews, what looked like it might once have been an almandine pastry of some sort, but which now looked like mush, and half a dozen black-and-white gibbous moon biscuits, which Eloise had always thought tasted so good that Chef must fashion them from flour, sugar (white and brown), treacle, stevia, rice malt, love, and weak magic. How else could she have gotten that incredible taste? Eloise gave her friend another hug, and mouthed a silent, "Thank you so much."

She closed the bag, set it on the far side of her cot, and stared at it. It all looked so wonderful.

And it was all completely forbidden to her.

The right thing to do would be to give it back to Jerome, explain why, and ask him to remove the temptation. Or she could keep it, so she did not offend him, and give it to Märgärët to remove. Or she could try to hide it, but not eat it, because she wasn't supposed to.

Stuff it, thought Eloise. She'd just had a needle jammed into her hand, she was being deliberately starved, every moment with the baroness was one form of unpleasantness or another, and every moment away from her involved working her behind off. Johanna had broken the rules by going to her garden. So, by her own reckoning, Eloise deserved a treat. And here it was.

She grabbed the bag, set it on her lap, and pulled out a gibbous moon biscuit.

While Eloise ate, alternating between a bite of the glorious biscuits and a bite of something more sensible, Jerome moved around the room in a way that was typical of his curious approach to the world. He walked along the edge of Eloise's cot on his two back legs, then his two front legs, then his back ones again. He shimmied up the table leg, dangled upside down from the table top, jumped to the chair, then to the floor, then up onto Eloise's bedside table where he picked up, examined, and put down each item like it was a museum artifact from a bygone era. Then he dropped back to the floor, scurried up the leg of Johanna's cot, again balanced himself on two feet walking along its edge, and then—very cheeky—flopped onto the middle of her pillow like he was going to have a nap.

He heard the scroll rustle under the pillow. "Hey, what have we here?"

Eloise waved her hands for him to leave it alone, but that was not Jerome's way. He grabbed and unfurled it. "What's this supposed to be, El?" He turned the scroll around for her to see.

She knew she was breaking some sort of rule by just looking at it. Or was she? Jerome was the one who'd gotten it out. He was the one who'd unrolled it. He was the one holding it, and he was the one who showed it to her. Her eyes just happened to be pointing in the right direction.

She moved closer to him, leaned over, and looked carefully.

The hemp parchment had an image that looked like a scholar's drawing of a body. It was a girl depicted as if she were lying on the ground, arms and legs out like she was making a snow angel. Fourteen lines poked out of her, and two hovered above her head with question marks next to them. Along one edge was a list of 16 words, which Eloise could not read—the handwriting seemed to be archaic squiggles. The lines drawn on the snow angel protruded from different parts of her face, hands, and neck. Each had a word written near it in the unfamiliar scrawl, as well as a crudely drawn line of drops of something descending from it. Blood, probably, since they started at the point where the lines touched the body.

"Really, Elbow, what's this supposed to be? Is this what you're supposed to do in the ceremony?"

Eloise shrugged, and wrote, *I have no idea.*

"I wouldn't do this for all the olives in the Eastern Lands, all the tundra in the Central Ranges, or all the haggleberry tea in The South. Well, maybe for the tea. If it was the right tea. But this is nuts."

Eloise nodded grim agreement.

The door burst open, slamming against the wall. Märgärët stormed in, eyes raging. Jerome froze in shock. Eloise scrambled backward away from them both, scattering the remaining contraband food.

"You!" she snarled at Jerome. "Drop that and get out! Never enter this room again."

Jerome looked at Eloise, unsure. Why was a servant telling him what to do? Eloise nodded.

Jerome scampered up the wall, his tail flicking mute chipmunk insults as he went, and exited through the high window.

Märgärët grabbed Eloise by the upper arm. "You will come and explain yourself to the baroness. Now!"

Eloise tried to free herself, but Märgärët held fast, yanking her from the room.

ONE GOOD REASON

The walk of shame to the baroness's rooms took Eloise through the heart of the castle. Embarrassment burned her cheeks and she could have sworn that when she passed the Receiving Room, her mother, who was talking to her First Advisor, looked up long enough to shake her head disapprovingly.

Märgärët took her to a room Eloise had never seen before. She knew the door, but had never seen it unlocked. She'd always assumed it was disused storage, being relatively close to the kitchen. Far from it. It was an antechamber of such opulence that Eloise was astounded she'd never heard it mentioned before. Tapestries depicting an unfamiliar queen's coronation filled two walls. The other walls in the windowless room were lined in wood the color of an almost-black ale her father sometimes had as a treat. The floor was not stone, but wood, made of pieces cut to rectangles and squares of uniform width and length, and laid so they fit together in a geometric mosaic. Few rooms in the castle had floors like this: only her parents' bedroom, the First Advisor's office, and the Salon de Dance. Guttering candles set before mirrors competed with a lit fireplace to cast flickering light over the deep-pillowed armchairs and precisely placed stonewood tables. A side table held a crystal pitcher of water and an overflowing bowl of off-season fruits brought in from Çalaht knew where.

"I can hear you gawping. Stop it." The gruff voice came from one of two comfortable chairs set facing the fireplace. The Thorning Master's claw-headed cane leaned against the one on the left, and Eloise could see a crone's hands balancing a teacup and saucer. There was a shake in them she did not remember seeing before. "Stand where I can see you."

Eloise moved to the right of the fireplace and faced Baroness Stúüùbenhocker. She kept her eyes lowered, looking at the old woman's feet rather than her face. Once again, a long silence lingered. Eloise found it hard not to fidget. She concentrated on counting the pieces in the parquetry floor. It was better than looking at the torture ring, more interesting. The way they fit together appealed to her. Eloise heard the quiet chink of cup against saucer several times, but no sipping sounds.

"Look me in the eyes, child."

Eloise raised her gaze to the Thorning Master's face, and they locked eyes. In the firelight, the old woman's ash-colored eyes had a slight cloudiness across them. Eloise wondered if the baroness would live long enough for complete blindness to steal her sight. It was an uncharitable thought.

The Thorning Master humphed and set the cup and saucer on the small table between the two chairs. "You are completely unprepared for this. Were you not told what was coming?"

Eloise shook her head.

"You may speak. I'm not sure there's much point in holding you to silence, given where things stand."

Eloise had spent so long trying to suppress the urge to speak, using words voluntarily now struck her as awkward.

"No, Baroness Stúüùbenhocker. Our queen did not speak of the Thorning Ceremony at all."

"That would be about right."

Eloise wanted to ask what that meant, but did not feel she was in any position to request explanations. She was there to give them.

"Let me ask you a question," the Thorning Master said. "Do I strike you as stupid?"

"No, Baroness."

"Blind? Incapable? Enfeebled? Perhaps two coins short of a full tithe?"

"No, Baroness."

"I should think rather not. Which is what puzzles me about what you have done." She took another shaky sip of tea. "Show me the wound."

Eloise untied the linen strip that held a gauze piece in place. The wound stung still from the ointment that Märgärët had used. Eloise extended her hand, and the old woman grasped it with her index finger and thumb, tilting the hand so it was easier to see in the firelight. "A clean job." Eloise was not sure if she meant the way Märgärët had tended the wound or the way the Thorning Master herself had created it.

She let go the hand and picked up her cup and saucer. Another slow, shaky sip, then she put the cup back down and pointed to the other chair. "Sit."

Eloise sat, staying as far away as she could.

"There is not a lot of call for what I do," she said. "How many females are in line for the throne in a generation? And yet here I am. I've been doing it a long time." Her fingers drummed slowly on the armrest. Her gaze stayed locked on Eloise, whether Eloise looked at her or not. "Your mother's Thorning Ceremony..." She moved her hand to her cane head. "Well, that's a matter of public record, a record that I'm sure has found its way to an unlikely box or corner somewhere."

Eloise had no idea what that meant.

"I said on the day you were introduced to me that the Thorning Ceremony reveals. For your mother, it revealed control, determination, and a certain coldness. You are likely unsurprised."

Yes, that was her mother.

"Your grandmother. That was another matter. She attacked the ceremony," said the baroness. "Placed the thorns as fast as Protocol allowed. From her Thorning Ceremony, you would have expected her to be a strong, decisive queen." The old woman closed her eyes, sighing. "If only her heart had been as resilient as the rest of her." Another long sip of tea. "I was already twice Märgärët's age when I was your grandmother's Thorning Master." She gave a dry chuckle. The sound surprised Eloise, who had thought the baroness completely devoid of humor. "The last thing you want is a green Thorning Master. Anyway, what your grandmother's Thorning Ceremony revealed, alas, was a propensity toward self-harm, in all its many shapes. This became clear to me when the marriage to your grandfather was announced. A disaster from the moment they met." She shook her head, reliving it. "Your great-grandmother's was my first Thorning Ceremony." She gave another dry chuckle. "Trust me, you really don't want a Thorning Master who was as nervous as I was. I felt sorry for her."

Eloise looked at the fire, wondering what any of this had to do with her. It was interesting, sort of, but she didn't know why the old crust was telling her all this. Baroness Stúüùbenhocker seemed to be lost in some sort of reverie.

Plus, what she said raised all kinds of questions, like what in the world happened at her mother's ceremony? And how was the baroness even still alive if she'd been Eloise's great-grandmother's Thorning Master? Did she have some sort of weak magic for simply not dying? Was such a thing even possible? Eloise didn't think so. Maybe she was just a tough old battle axe.

The baroness snapped her fingers in front of Eloise's face, bringing her back to the room. "That, right there. That is your problem. One of them, anyway. There are others." She leaned back in her chair and idly twisted one of the thorns that pierced her neck. Eloise had seen her do this before with that particular thorn, and it gave her the willies. "Your biggest problem, of course, is whether or not you'll be allowed to continue your training."

There was no "of course" about it. Eloise had not considered the possibility that she would not be allowed to participate.

The baroness continued. "Another of your problems is that you don't seem to think my rules apply to you. Speaking. Entertaining your friend. Eating that which was not provided. Not following instruction. Shall I continue?"

"No, Baroness."

"Are you sure you're firstborn? I have never conducted a Thorning Ceremony for twins, but I have done sisters. Princess Johanna seems much more suited to this. And yet, they tell me that should you succeed, you will be named Future Ruler and Heir. The ways of Çalaht are shrouded. Certainly in this case."

There was nothing to say to that.

"Pour me another cup of tea."

"Yes, Baroness." Eloise picked up the cup from the table and took it to the sideboard. The last thing she felt like doing was waiting on her. But she'd do so perfectly, if for no other reason than for her own dignity. Eloise felt the side of the teapot. Still hot. Eloise took a fresh cup and filled it three-quarters full so it would not spill when the baroness's hands shook. It was not haggleberry tea, but what smelled like ginger. More medicinal than haggleberry. Did the Thorning Master have stomach woes? Perhaps that was the source of her dyspeptic manner. Eloise also took a dessert plate and filled it with a selection of the fruits—a sprig of grapes (her favorites, after brunchberries), a few blueberries (also her favorites after grapes and brunchberries), two of the nicest strawberries she'd seen in months, and a dried fig. Eloise couldn't help thinking that if she poked the fig with a few toothpicks, it would resemble the baroness fairly closely. She placed the tea and plate on the table next to her chair, then resumed standing where she had originally.

The Thorning Master looked at the tea and plate, then up at Eloise, who this time looked her straight in the eye. "I see. Interesting." She picked up a strawberry, looked at it, then set it down again. She did the same with the fig and the grapes. "Tell me, child. Do you wish to continue?"

She knew what the answer should be. She ought to say, "Yes, of course." But those words would not come. Not easily, or with full heart. She forced herself to say them anyway. "Yes, of course, Baroness."

"Why?"

"Why?" Eloise was unprepared for the question, so she said the first thing that came to mind, which happened to be the truth. "Because they expect it of me."

"I see. Is that adequate?"

"Adequate?"

"Is meeting the expectations of others an adequate reason?"

"I don't know what to say to that. It is expected."

"What would they do if you refused? Banish you? Gossip about you? Force you to do it anyway? Punish you? Toss you in the dungeon?"

"You say there is a choice, but there is not. I am firstborn. I will be named Future Ruler and Heir. It is not up to me. Such is Protocol."

"You were told you had a choice when you first started. That choice remains."

"On matters like this, there is no real choice. Shall I be recorded as one of the ones who did not go through the Thorning Ceremony? No, it is not up to me."

"You are wrong there. Sure, there are expectations. But I assure you that 'Protocol says' is never enough justification for anything. Nothing at all. In this matter, and if I can give you a coin and a half's worth of advice, in *all* matters, you had best know your 'why.' Your particular reason." She leaned forward. "I tell you what. There is, at this point, exactly one good reason for you to do this, to go through the Thorning Ceremony. Work it out, then convince me it applies to you. Give me this reason why you would choose to continue, and I shall consider allowing you to carry on. But think fast. I have little time to waste on this."

Eloise felt herself in a double bind. She did not want to walk away, because that would just be too embarrassing. But she also did not feel compelled to participate. In fact, the whole thing struck her as repugnant. Poking herself with thorns? For Çalaht's sake, what was the point?

So, what did she mean by "one good reason?" Following Protocol was not enough. Meeting expectations was wrong. She doubted doing it to please her mother was what the baroness had in mind. So what, then?

While Eloise thought, the baroness picked through the plate of fruits, taking half bites of each, the various thorns stuck through her face animating her movements. This struck Eloise as a particularly strange way to eat. Stranger still was the old woman's tongue. Eloise had not seen it before, but there was a small thorn in there as well. It did not affect her speech, but it must have caused incredible discomfort when it was first put there. She must have an extremely high tolerance for pain. Or incredible discipline. Maybe both. Or maybe she just did it because she could.

That's when Eloise realized what Old Pincushion must mean. Eloise had to do it for herself, not others. The point was to prove in her own mind (and body) that she was able to conquer the task. She'd heard about people who did extreme things, like walking across hot coals, lying on beds made of needles, or fasting for a month. The point was to push past it to see what was possible, to master one's aversions, one's doubts, and one's fears to achieve what previously had seemed impossible.

She got it in her head, but it was a different matter to get it in her gut. She thought of Johanna, blithely poking the needle into herself like she'd been doing it forever. Märgärët was the same, placing needle after needle, and, Eloise suspected, when she on her own and with the baroness's permission, working with thorns. Clearly Old Pincushion had mastered it many times over. Eloise was nowhere close. For her to do this, she'd have to get past her tendency to faint, increase her tolerance for pain, and actually want to.

Eloise shifted. "I think I get it. I have to prove to myself that I can do it. It is for me. Not Protocol, and not others. Me."

The Thorning Master set down half a strawberry and folded her hands. "Correct."

"I would like to continue, please."

"Based on what?"

"Based on a lot of things. If generations of Gumballs have done it, then it must be doable. You've said yourself that my mother did it, my grandmother did it, and my great-grandmother. So it is doable. I cannot imagine that they were so very different to me. If it was possible for them, it is possible for me. I can't say I crave continuing. I can't even really say that 'I want to' is the right choice of words. I think I need to. For me. So I know that I can do it."

"I see," said the baroness. "I see." She looked hard at Eloise and let one of her silences sit between them. Eloise looked at the woman's face, and occupied the silence by counting the number of piercings. "Dozens" shaped itself into a specific number: 256 in the face and neck alone. Impressive, in its own way.

The Thorning Master broke the silence. "You will hold your silence? You will adhere to my rules? You will submit fully, with humility and willingness?"

"Yes, Baroness."

"Very well then. You will return to the seclusion room and stay until called. Your silence resumes now."

Eloise nodded.

"I have a last word of advice for you, Princess Eloise Hydra Gumball III." The Thorning Master's ashen eyes bore into her. "Buck up. Truly, child. Buck up."

Eloise nodded again.

"Dismissed."

❦ 14 ❦

WEEDING DEVIL'S GRASS

Johanna shoved her hands into the dirt, scrabbling for the root of the devil's grass runner that dared threaten her carrot patch. The stuff could (and would) sprout up from the tiniest broken sliver left behind. She followed the line of root as it snaked below the surface of the garden, careful to pull it out without breaking any of it off—tricky at the best of times, but even harder now when she was as upset as she was.

This Thorning Ceremony thing was getting up her nose. Why was she even doing it? What was the point? Eloise was going to be named heir, being firstborn. Sure, Protocol said that all girls in line for the throne had to do it, but to what end?

But Eloise was bad at it all. So very bad. Embarrassingly so. Johanna felt for her sister. She knew Eloise had her peculiar ways, what she called her "habits." Her inability to do what the Thorning Master was asking of them was probably tied to those habits, somehow. But still... to have fainted? To be unable to prick her finger with the tiniest of healing needles? It was a bit pathetic. But there was nothing she could do for Eloise. She'd have to find her own way.

There! She found the beginning of the root line. She carefully pulled the devil's grass root at both ends, removing it from the ground toward the middle. It came free in a single piece. Good. The stuff was Çalaht-cursed, and the sooner it was rotting in the compost heap, the better.

Seventeen minutes. That was the age difference between Eloise and herself. Seventeen minutes that defined her life. Seventeen minutes between being a queen someday and not.

She put the devil's grass weed at the bottom of an empty compost bay, grabbed a shovel, and began turning the heap in the next bay over onto the weed. The heat would cook it, making sure it never threatened her carrots again. Shovelful after shovelful, she buried what was once a problem, and which now would decay into a useful contributor to her garden.

She paused, mid-heave. She was turning a negative into a positive, with the help of nature.

A negative into a positive. A negative into a positive. The idea rattled around in her head the way that song "Three Bags of Groats for My Sweetheart" would if you let it. She finished turning the pile.

She was still thinking "negative into a positive" as she grabbed the tongs she used to tend her haggleberry bush. Its fruit was near ripe, which meant its leaves would be at their sharpest to protect the indigo berries. Johanna had learned it was also when the plant seemed to like an extra helping of food. Lucerne, if she had it, or maybe a green manure of some sort, like clover or vetch. All three, if she could. Which she could. It was her favorite of all her plants.

She gathered a mixed armload of dried clippings of the three plants, which she kept in piles next to the compost bays. The load was extra generous, making it hard to see the plant as she approached it.

Careful not to get too close, she dropped the pile by the spot where she'd work. Using the tongs, Johanna placed generous piles of mulch around the base of the bush, not so close that it would threaten to rot the main stem, but close enough to make it easy for the roots to suck the mulch's goodness.

Negative into a positive. How could she turn a negative into a positive here?

She completed the circle of mulch with a little to spare. Holstering her tongs, she used her hands to scoop up the last bits of lucerne, clover, and vetch. She reached the handful forward to get in near the base.

She came too close. The haggleberry defended itself as nature intended, a leaf slicing into the back of Johanna's hand, embedding itself into her.

It hurt, but she knew it was her own fault. *Sorry, baby*, she thought to the plant. *Did I get too close?*

Johanna withdrew her hand and examined the leaf that poked out of it. It looked like one of the baroness's thorns.

And it didn't bother her. Not in the least. Sure, it stung a little, and she was bleeding, but she didn't care. It came from a plant she loved, so she could take it. No problem.

In that moment, she knew the Thorning Ceremony was something that she could do. She just had to treat the thorns like leaves from her haggleberry plant. Make them no big deal.

Johanna thought about the passage from the *Livre de Protocol* that they'd read what seemed like years ago. "Ye shall pierceth the flesh—scalp, face, neck, and hands—of the most honored maidens, and name from among them the Heir." It was the first time she'd really considered the words.

"Name from among them the Heir." She had always assumed that the firstborn would be named heir. That's just the way things always were. But what if the firstborn was not the best choice? What if someone else, maybe someone just 17 minutes younger than the firstborn, was better suited to being named future ruler and heir? The text of the *Livre* seemed not to preclude it.

That's how she would turn her negative into a positive. She'd just be better than Eloise. She'd make it obvious that she was the better choice. She would do the best Thorning Ceremony anyone had ever done, whatever that meant. She'd be better at the preparation. She'd be better at whatever Old Pincushion asked her to do. She'd be better at all of it, and whoever it was who named the heir would have no choice but to pick her.

The wrought-iron gate to her secret garden rattled, then rattled again. "How dare you!" It was Märgärët. "Come out of there this instant!"

Slowly, Johanna stood and silently thanked the haggleberry bush, its leaf still embedded in the back of her hand. Moving deliberately while Märgärët fumed outside, Johanna put back the tongs, wiped dirt from her hands, picked up her gardening basket, and walked toward the servant. With each step, Johanna gathered her determination, creating a reservoir of resolve. By the time she unlocked the gate and put herself back in the control of the scowling young woman, Johanna was ready to face whatever came next.

And to do it better than Eloise could ever dream of.

❧ 15 ❧

BAWLED OUT

When Märgärët returned Eloise to the Seclusion Room, Johanna was still not there. "Where is the princess?" she demanded.

Eloise shook her head. There was no way she'd give Johanna up.

"Suit yourself. I'll find her on my own." The servant closed the door, and once again, there was the scratch of a key and the click of a door lock.

An hour later, Märgärët opened the door and shoved Johanna in. "My leaving the door unlocked was a courtesy. That courtesy will no longer be extended. I'll repeat the baroness's words: 'This is my third instruction: you will go to the room where you will be secluded. You will not leave it unless I explicitly give you permission. You will have minimal or no contact with castle and Court, except as directed by me.' Which part of that was unclear?"

She left without waiting for an answer.

Johanna paced their small room, clasping her hands in front of her, then behind, eyes dark. Eloise signed a question mark.

Johanna's reply was almost unintelligible because of her fury. *Mtb bawled me out for going to garden.*

Eloise guessed that "Mtb" was "Märgärët the something-starting-with-b." Bellicose? Bombast? Betrayer? Not important. *How bad?* she replied.

Took my [indistinct gesture]. *Said never do it again.*

Eloise mimicked the gesture she didn't understand and added a question mark.

Johanna exaggerated her reply. *Gardening basket.*

Oh. Ouch.

She can jump up my [indistinct gesture] *and* [indistinct gesture]. *I hate her.*

Eloise mouthed a silent, "Sorry."

Mtb took me to BS. She also chewed me out.

"BS." That would be "Baroness Stúüùbenhocker." *Terrible?*

Threatened to chuck me out of the training and not let me do TC.

So Johanna had received a lecture from Old Pincushion, too, including the same threat of exclusion.

Johanna drew a question mark in the air and pointed at her sister. Eloise wasn't sure what she was asking, and even after Johanna's confession, she was embarrassed to admit what had happened to her.

Johanna picked up her scroll, waggled it at Eloise and made another question mark.

Of course. Johanna saw that the scroll was not only moved from where she had left it, but unrolled.

Sorry, I looked, said Eloise.

What!? Why!? That was mine! You weren't supposed to!

I know, I know. Sorry.

You really shouldn't have done that. That was wrong.

I got caught looking at it. Didn't really get that good of a look, said Eloise. It wasn't strictly the truth, but it wasn't something Johanna would be able to test either way.

Mtb?

Yes. Plus, Jerome was here too.

J? How?

Eloise pointed to the window. *With food.*

Çalaht's bunions, El. You did, what, three things you weren't allowed all to at once. Are you trying to get us into trouble?

That's a bit rich coming from someone who left the room to go check plants.

I only broke one rule. Johanna examined her scroll to see if it was damaged or changed. *So what did Mtb do?*

Dragged me to BS. She threatened me with no TC. I had to convince her not to turf me out.

So did I.

Eloise sat on her cot. *Did you get a talk about "Why?"*

Why? What why?

BS lectured me about "Knowing your why."

No. I got a lecture about "Proper respect for rules and process and boundaries." Such bull [indistinct gesture].

The door unlocked, and at once, the girls dropped their hands to their laps. Märgärët came in carrying a board, a hammer, and a small pail of nails. Without looking at either of them, she climbed up onto the table, which was still where Eloise had moved it, and nailed the board across the window. A sliver of light could still come through above and below the board, but the room was now permanently darker, and there was no way the window would open again without proper tools.

When Märgärët was done, she stepped down, looked at Eloise, and said simply, "No visitors. I would have thought that rule was clear. Apparently not." Then she left, locking the door again.

Prison, signed Eloise.

I hate them both. But you didn't help.

Neither did you.

Johanna rolled up the scroll and slipped it back under her pillow. Eloise felt the awkwardness between them. She really shouldn't have looked at the scroll. Or eaten the food. Or had a visitor. But Johanna had transgressed as well, for longer. A mess, all around.

Johanna looked at her, and Eloise signed, *Feel like quitting.* It was going to be a statement, but at the last moment, she added a question mark.

Johanna scrunched her face into an "Are you crazy?" look. [Indistinct gesture] *that and* [indistinct gesture] *them. I'm gonna show them. Mtb and BS both!*

Me too. But Eloise didn't really feel it.

Johanna paced the room while Eloise lay on her cot. Every now and again, she poked the spot in her hand where the baroness's needle had gone in, as though she needed to make sure it was still sore.

The twins passed the rest of the afternoon in restless silence, each reliving their encounter with the Thorning Master and the circumstances that had led to it. At one point, Märgärët brought them some thin miso soup, shot them both disdainful looks, and literally "tisked" out loud. She also stopped behaving like a servant in any way. Where previously she had served their food, the girls were left to dish up the watery meal themselves. At least she made sure the fire in the fireplace was going. Eloise didn't know if she could reliably light one on her own.

She spent the night mulling over the Thorning Master's phrase, "You must know your 'why.'" It echoed in her head. Intellectually, Eloise understood that she needed to prove it to herself. She had to toughen up, get used to ramming thorns into herself, and then stand in front of Court and just go through with it all. But she didn't want to. She didn't feel the need in her guts, and she doubted she ever would.

And that scared her almost as much as the needles and thorns did.

16

FROM DERVISH ELDER TO
CHOKE LILY

The next day, Märgärët collected them and took them to work with the dyer and his bubbling vats of color (Eloise ended up with one hand splattered yellow and the other splashed an unattractive lime green), then later escorted them to the Torture Tower. The table had three stools at it, in addition to the usual one for the baroness.

Once they were seated, the Thorning Master placed a sheet of hemp parchment and a needle in front of each of them. "You may take notes. I say things once."

Eloise looked for quill and ink. There were none. The baroness began to speak, and she saw Märgärët prick her left thumb with the needle, squeeze it to produce a drop of blood, dip the needle in it, then begin to jot words on her sheet.

They were supposed to take notes in their own blood? Eloise could imagine some twisted logic that said they needed to get used to poking themselves, but Eloise had no interest in that. She fished a piece of chalk from her apron pocket. Perhaps that would work. She focused her attention on what the baroness was saying, trying to commit it to memory in case her note-taking failed.

"Broadly, there are two things you need to know. First, the thorns and their effects. Second, where the thorns are placed, and their order. While there are traditions around which thorns go where, Protocol allows discretion. In other words, it will be your choice. And what you choose will not only be copied down by the scribes, it will also be gossiped about by everyone—not that that matters. But you should expect it."

The baroness reached into her drawer and removed a hessian pouch dyed black. She slid out four bundles of gray linen, each tied closed with a coal-black ribbon. She placed one in front of herself and one in front of each of the girls. Following the baroness's lead, Eloise untied the precise bow and placed the roll flat on the table. Inside each were pairs of thorns. Eloise looked at each of the different thorn types and tried to imagine shoving them into her hand the way the baroness had done. The thought made her woozy. The room started to sway.

The Thorning Master's bamboo switch smacked the table near Eloise's thorns. "Stay present, child."

Startled, Eloise nodded.

The baroness took a moment to arrange her thorn pairs, and Eloise glanced over to see Märgärët sketching them on her parchment. She was amazed. Using just stipples and lines of her blood, and despite the fact that the coarse hemp parchment leached the fluid, the servant girl had captured the thorns' nuances—their shapes, widths, lengths, sharpnesses, bends, and barbs. What could she do with charcoal or watercolors? It was a side of her Eloise had not expected.

Eloise then looked at Johanna. Her sister had not yet pricked her thumb, but she held the needle poised, and looked like she was steeling herself to do it at any moment.

Eloise picked up her own needle and rolled it between her middle finger and thumb, considering. Maybe, just maybe, if she was careful not to poke it in too far, she could do it. She placed it on the fleshiest part of the thumb, pressing a little. Her skin resisted, then gave way. The point broke through. The pain was everything Eloise had expected, and she whipped the needle out, sucking in air through her teeth. A small bead of blood formed on the surface, hardly enough to write a single letter. How was Märgärët getting enough to do art, much less take notes?

The Thorning Master picked up the first pair of thorns, which were long and had a hook at one end. "Strictly speaking, the scholars and boffins will tell you this is not a thorn, but a spine. Pick up one of yours and carefully graze your skin to get a sense of its sharpness. Märgärët, you may place one of yours."

Eloise picked up a hook-shaped thorn between her thumb and index finger and carefully grazed it across the back of her hand. It left a small scratch. Märgärët, however, took hers and hooked it into the flesh of her neck. Eloise, unready for the sudden piercing, fainted.

She came to, coughing from the smell of the reviving vial Märgärët held under her nose. The hooked thorn still dangled from her neck. Eloise shook her head to clear it and sat back on her stool.

"If you are going to faint every time anyone does something like that, this is going to take a very, very long time. Buck up, Princess Eloise." The Thorning Master said her name like it was coated in lemons. "To continue, this spine comes from a plant found in The South called Çalaht's knitter, for reasons that have less to do with the Divine One, and more to do with the fact that croftwomen use immature versions to crochet winter garments, especially hooded wind sweaters. In mature spines, the tip is as sharp as any in the set, which makes it relatively easy to insert. However, see this barb? It prevents the thorn from going backward. That means it must be removed by pushing it all the way through. It is hard to see, but the sides of the mature ones are serrated. You should expect that to be uncomfortable. Märgärët, please remove your... Eloise, don't faint!"

Eloise gripped the table, watching Märgärët pull the long end of the thorn through her neck, removing it. A trickle of blood dripped. Even though Märgärët hid it, Eloise could tell it hurt like the blazes.

Next, the baroness held up two woody thorns about half as long as her index finger. "From the Eastern Lands comes the thorny olive. Scratch the back of your hand with it. Märgärët, place yours."

Eloise picked one up and carefully drew it across the back of her hand, keeping her eyes away from the servant. Where the thorn touched her hand, an angry, red welt blossomed, itching horribly. She looked up and saw that Märgärët had put hers into the middle of her forehead. She looked like the realm's worst echidna. Or perhaps the world's worst rhino.

"The fruits of the thorny olive are some of the largest, most desirable olives that grow anywhere," said the baroness. "So nature had to find a way for the plant to protect its bounty. Her solution was these, some of the most aggressive thorns found in all the realms. They pierce with exceeding ease and cause the itch that you are feeling now. You should expect them, too, to be... uncomfortable.

"Nature was, however, perverse," continued the baroness. "The prick of the thorn, as you will no doubt be experiencing right now, induces a craving for olives. So the plant doesn't just protect itself from those who would pluck its fruit, it lures them to damage themselves as well, preventing them from doing so in the future."

Now that she mentioned it, Eloise was definitely feeling peckish for olives. "Craving" was probably too strong, but maybe it was mild because she had not fully put the thorn into her skin. The unexpected yearning for olives seemed ludicrous. But there it was.

"That desire cannot be sated by actually eating olives. You could eat a barrel of them and ask for a second. So I don't suggest you ever try. You must simply tolerate the desire until it dissipates. Which it will."

Olive bread, thought Eloise, stomach rumbling. *Olive pie. Olive couscous. Olive tapenade. Olive risotto. Olive pesto. Olive kebabs. Olive salsa. Olive salad. Olive platter. Olive antipasto. Olive frittata. Roasted olives. Braised olives. Baked olives. Olive purée. Olive muffins. Olive cake. Olive mousse.*

Thwack!

The slap of bamboo in the middle of the table brought Eloise back to the room. "The craving will pass," said the Thorning Master. "Just give it time."

Eloise and Johanna both nodded. Märgärët dabbed the corners of her mouth with the back of her hand, and swallowed back saliva.

Eloise knew the next one before the Thorning Master said anything. It was the familiar spike of choke lily. The choke lily was a virulent grower, normally found in the shallows of mangrove swamps, where they were controlled by muskrats, who valued them as a delicacy—especially the flower petals plucked from around the plant's central spike. A century before, a homesick muskrat, despatched from The South as an ambassador, planted one in a secluded part of a lake three strong lengths beyond the castle walls. The plant had taken over, its spikes rendering the water unfit for habitation or recreation. It instantly became a must-see on the muskrat tourist maps for all the realms. The body of water was soon known as Choke Lily Lake, and the plant's blossoms were known to muskrats everywhere as the best in all the realms.

"The choke lily thorn is one of the easier in the set to place," said the baroness. "It can be inserted and removed with ease, similar to a healing needle, and its only side effect is inducing thirst."

Eloise hadn't known that about the plant. It explained why muskrats always had water packs with them when they made their pilgrimage to the lake, which had always struck her as counterintuitive. Eloise scratched the back of her hand with the choke lily thorn. She thought that perhaps she might feel a little thirsty, but was not sure. Maybe it required piercing the skin.

Eloise also recognized the next thorn—a spiked spinner from the dervish elder. She had been fascinated by the dervish elder half a decade before, when her family made a trip to one of the royal family holdings in the Kestrel Mountains near the border between the realms of the Western Lands and All That Really Matters and the Central Ranges. There was a dervish elder forest there, and they had timed their visit for what the locals called "spinning season," when the elders let loose a rain of winged seeds that spun like tops in the wind. The seeds spun and flew until the winds that bore them abated, and they wound their way downward, impaling their spikes into the dirt below. If conditions were just right, roots would sprout from the spike and a new dervish elder would grow. Eloise clearly remembered standing beneath a parasol under the dark, whirling cloud of seeds, fascinated by nature's display of aerial acrobatics.

When she scratched herself with the spinner, she felt, as the baroness had said she would, a mild dizziness.

The Thorning Master picked up the next one. "Again, take this and scrape the back of your other hand."

Eloise picked up one of the thorns. It was a handspan long, deep brown, and straight as a needle. When she scraped the back of her right hand, it, too, raised an angry, red welt. Instead of an itch, it burned like a line of sparks had landed on her. Märgärët poked hers into the top of her head.

"These are firethorns, from here in the Western Lands and All That Really Matters. As you are feeling now, they are well named. When they pierce, they light a fire in your skin that stays with you for a day and a night once removed, if not treated with aloe. That is why aloe vera is part of the Wisdom Salve placed on one after the ceremony."

Next were two thorns three times the length of the firethorns, nasty and bone white. "Hold the point to the palm of your hand," said the old woman.

When Eloise did that, she felt her palm tingle, and then nothing. The spot went numb.

"These are thorns of the deadman's bush of the Half Kingdom. They are, in a sense, the opposite of the firethorns. Where they pierce, they create numbness—dead man's flesh, if you will. It lasts as long as the thorn has contact, and disappears a few seconds to a minute after it is removed. The length of time depends on the freshness of the thorn, the site of its placing, and the depth of the piercing."

It was true. When Eloise removed the thorn, feeling returned within less than a minute. She tried it again on other spots on her hand. The change from feeling to numbness and back was eerie and disconcerting.

She risked a glance at Märgärët, who had skewered a flap of skin in her hand. Eloise managed not to swoon.

"It is unlikely that you will ever encounter this next one in the wild," said Stúüùbenhocker. The thorn she held up was unlike any of the others—wispy and thin, with seven strands like a horsetail cloud. "This comes from the barking vine lotus. Pick one of yours up by the central stem and avoid touching the threads. Now place a finger near it, like this." The baroness held her index finger pointing upward below the thorn's strings. She then lowered it toward her finger. The strands of the horsetail slowly closed around her finger like a sea anemone. Eloise did the same. It felt like she was being grabbed by the tiniest of octopus suckers. Its sting was light, almost a tickle.

"Do not be fooled by its gentle touch. Try to remove your finger."

It wouldn't let go. The harder Eloise pulled, the tighter it held on, invisible barbs digging in.

"To release yourself, you do the opposite of what instinct would tell you. You must push further in, go deeper, to trigger a release."

It worked. As soon as Eloise moved her finger far enough into the barking vine lotus, the seven strands let go. They left behind the smallest pinpricks of blood where they'd been attached, but otherwise, there was no lasting consequence. At least, none that was obvious.

Last, the baroness unwrapped two thorns from a cloth on their own within the linen roll. "These two are perhaps the most difficult of all, and they are not in the set I have given you. The plant is nicknamed mad monk's breakfast, and the thorns are the smallest of the lot. They are dull, which makes it hard for them to pierce the skin. But once they do, they change how you feel. What that change is depends on you, both your nature and the place where you've put them. I've known them to cause deep despair—so much so that one lass ran from the hall and tried to drown herself in a trough. But I've also known them to induce uncontrolled giggling or profound awe. It is unpredictable, and can be... uncomfortable." She placed them back on the cloth and wiped her hand on her robe. "Choose where you place them with care. It will matter to you, it will be recorded, and it will be commented upon, as I said."

The old woman straightened in her chair. "So, it is obvious that the thorns represent the different regions. There is one plant indigenous to each of the four-and-a-half realms. The Commentaries to the *Livre de Protocol* go on and on about this for a tedious eternity. But, to my mind, there are other, more significant, and much older associations to make. These I celebrate, and will now enumerate." One by one, she picked up the thorns and spoke to them. "The thorny olive is the earth, the land that sustains us. The dervish elder's spinner is a true acrobat of the air. The firethorn burns like the fire it is named after. The choke lily rules the waters. The wisps of the barking vine lotus give us ether and spirit. The Çalaht's knitter is creation or life, while the deadman's bush is its mirror—death and destruction. Mad monk's breakfast celebrates the hints of magic that remain in our world. Some say it can awaken the magic within, although I've not seen any evidence of this." She looked at each of them. "Think on these things in the coming days as you get to know the thorns. Connect with these ancient meanings and try to ascertain how they might apply to you. For they will. Care for these practice thorns. Guard them. Get to know them. And bring them with you from now on."

She let that hang for moment, then without another word, began her slow, painful descent down the tower stairs. Eloise studied her collection of 14 of the 16 thorns so intently that the eventual call of "Dismissed" barely registered.

17

STACKING WOOD

week, signed Eloise. *Until...*

Johanna nodded. *I don't feel ready.*

Eloise took a mouthful of miso broth. This time, there were shallots as well, sliced to razor thinness, and infinitesimally small shreds of tofu. In that moment, it was the best soup Eloise had ever tasted. It was like Chef was sending them a hug from the kitchens.

At least you can stab yourself at will, Eloise signed.

More to it than that.

I know. It was true. There was more to this thing than just putting pointy things through skin. It seemed like the Thorning Master had not yet covered key aspects to what they needed to know. Maybe they weren't worthy. Maybe Old Pincushion was just difficult. Whatever it was, the baroness was holding something back.

A week did not seem like much time at all, not when Eloise could barely bring herself to scratch her skin, much less place all the thorns. Johanna was definitely ahead in that department.

The soup break had been granted before the day's instruction. They had spent the morning stacking firewood. The wood mongers brought it to the kitchen in oversized carts and dumped it in a pile ten lengths from the kitchen door. She and Johanna had been given thick gloves and instructed how to stack it neatly in the woodshed, ready for Chef's use. Eloise guessed they had moved close to two strong weights worth of wood four to six split log pieces at a time.

Despite the tedium and the resulting sore muscles, Eloise much preferred wood stacking to sheet draping, polishing and cleaning bladed weapons, or any of the other tasks they'd been pressed into doing. At least with wood stacking, there were no dripping baskets, less need for extreme precision, little risk of losing fingers to sharp edges, not much chance of ending up with purple arms up to the elbows, and no supervision by hippos or other persnickety masters. There were no washer boys, ditch diggers, or blacksmith apprentices snickering and pointing behind her back. It was just her, the pieces of wood, and a shack to stack them in. The stacking was what she enjoyed—producing order from a jumbled chaos of wood. It suited her and soothed her habits with repetition and neatness. She and Johanna had started stacking at first light and had finished well after the castle's lunch bell had rung.

It was likely the Thorning Master's bamboo switch would get a workout that afternoon, given how tired Eloise felt.

One thing niggled at Eloise—the way Johanna had gone after the wood stacking. To Eloise, it was a task just to get done and do more or less well. But Johanna seemed to take it more seriously than that. It was like she was trying to race Eloise, to make her wood stack taller, neater, and more compact. Of course, nothing had been said, but as the morning wore on, Johanna seemed to speed up, not slow down, despite her fatigue. Part of Eloise was happy to let her sister sweat it out for what seemed like no reason. But another part of her sensed an underlying, unspoken challenge, a competitiveness that seemed out of character for her twin. Plus, Johanna did not want to share a single wood stack. She made it clear that she'd stack one side of the shed, and

Eloise could stack the other. That meant that it was clear who was doing more.

Challenge accepted, thought Eloise, and she, too, began to move faster and faster, until by the end of it they were both almost running from woodpile to shed and back, much to the wood monger's confusion.

To Eloise's eye, their competition ended in a draw when Märgärët came to pick them up, but it was weird that it had happened at all.

Something was going on with her sister. But what?

18

WHERE THE THORNS GO

Baroness Stúüùbenhocker was waiting impatiently for them that afternoon. The day was unseasonably warm, and blue, cloudless skies stretched as far as Eloise could see from all eight windows of the Torture Tower. It might have been nice to sit and stare idly at the purple-tinged mountains in the distance, and maybe listen to hear if the buzzing of the United Flower Pollinators Guild workers was audible from that high up. The UFPG were a particularly militant group, and wielded enormous influence within the realm, given their crucial role in everything from crops to ornamental flowers. The Guild motto was, "You don't really want to anger us bees, do you?" Eloise often listened to make sure their buzzing was audible, given how devastating a work stoppage from them might be.

The Thorning Master seemed unimpressed by the beauty of the day. She launched into her next lecture as if the first sentence followed on directly from the last one spoken the day before, and there hadn't been almost a full day and all that wood stacking in between.

Eloise, Johanna, and Märgärët sat at the table and spread out their thorn collections.

"There are, as we discussed, sixteen thorns, which means there are sixteen points on the body where they are placed," said the old woman once they had completed their staring at the iron rings. Eloise found that she could keep her mind where it was supposed to be much better than when they started, and the swish of bamboo was heard less frequently. "Where you choose to place them is up to you. It depends in part on what you think you can tolerate, as well as the meaning derived from the combination of thorn type and placement point. For example, if you place a deadman's bush where your third eye would be, it might be taken to mean that you wish to be numb to the insights of the Unseen. Or if you put the firethorn in the center of your throat near, the hollow of your neck, it could symbolize that your words will be incendiary. Similarly, a choke lily to the throat could mean you will drown people with words, or they are watery and ineffective. It all matters, and it is all on record, so choose wisely. But know this: there is no right way or wrong way. Plus, inevitably you will find a conflict between what you desire and what you have available. This is for you to resolve. Understood?"

They all nodded.

"So, where do you place them? One in each hand, directly in the center of the palms. One at the heart, one at the hollow of the throat, one at the wisdom eye in the middle of the forehead, one at the point at the top of the head, four in the neck—one either side of the throat, and one either side of the spine—one in each cheek, and one at each temple." As she listed the locations, she pointed to the thorns in her own body. "That leaves two that you may place at your discretion. In this way, no two Thorning Ceremonies are the same."

She picked up the two mad monk's breakfast thorns. "These are always last. They go last because the state they induce can be incapacitating. You would not want to miss out on the rest of the ceremony because your experience of mad monk's breakfast took you on a half day's journey to the La La Realms. You can place them in different spots, or you can combine their effects and place them together in one location. More than any other thorn, these are placed at your discretion. I've always favored the crown of the head, but that is personal preference. Be guided by your own instincts."

She gave them slates and chalk, had them draw the outline of a person, and then place the thorns on the picture indicating where they would go. Eloise spent a little too long making her drawing look real, so had to rush to position the thorns.

When they were done, the baroness shuffled her way around the table. She gave a satisfied nod at Märgärët's arrangement, a noncommittal head bob at Johanna's, but wrinkled her aggressively pierced nose at Eloise, adding a guttural, dismissive noise. "Did you think about this at all, or did you simply drop them in a jumble on your slate?"

Eloise felt blood rush to her cheeks.

"Try again. I'll wait."

Eloise felt the other three watching her as she cleared the thorns, then carefully placed them at the fourteen points on the drawing's body. She felt self-conscious, and worried she'd do it badly again, so she forced herself to move deliberately and consciously.

When she was done, the baroness gave her the same noncommittal head bob that Johanna got. Eloise took that as a sign of improvement.

The Thorning Master began a second shuffle around the table. She leaned over Märgärët's work, saying, "There is no right or wrong here, but consider swapping the dervish elder and the choke lily. See what difference that makes." Märgärët looked at her, then down at her slate, then back at the baroness. She nodded slowly, apparently achieving some understanding that Eloise could not fathom.

The old woman then moved to Johanna's chair. She considered the placement of the thorns, then leaned in and whispered something that only Johanna could hear. When the baroness moved toward Eloise, Johanna shook all the thorns from the slate and began rearranging them from scratch.

Old Pincushion spoke to Eloise. "I pity this person you've drawn. Look at how you have done the thorns." The baroness pointed at the slate.

"You have the dervish elder spinner poking out of the top of her crown. That would make her a wind-head, or maybe constantly dizzy. Not a good look. Next, the thorny olive is at her throat, which means everything she says would be an irritant. Your choke lily is at the heart, so she would forever thirst for love, but her heart would never be satisfied. The Çalaht's knitter is in the temple, which would not only bleed horribly, it would also be excruciating to push through and remove. Do you see what I mean? Where they go matters, both physically and symbolically. Try again."

Eloise placed her needles back on their cotton rest and considered them again. Märgärët and Johanna had both opened their scrolls and were referring to the diagram and its text. Her non-scrolled state suddenly seemed like a big deal. Sadly, there was nothing to be done. Eloise focused on trying to remember what each one did and where it could go that might make sense. After five attempts, she had an arrangement that the Thorning Master called "barely acceptable."

She'd take that. At least her poor drawn girl wouldn't be an unrequited, irritating, dizzy wind-head.

19

GOANNA SCAT SLURRY

Days later, the twins were spending the morning under the charge of the Master of Soil Conditioning, an irascible insect named Hërbërt de Dung Beetle. Master de Dung Beetle was responsible for the gathering, mixing, distribution, and application of fertilizers across all the realm's farms, and he knew more about soil improvement, fertilizer concoction, and plant growth promotion than anyone anywhere. He'd set the twins the task of shoveling goanna scat into a fertilizer slurry vat, mixing it with the bat and lemur scat already in there.

Both girls wore lavender-soaked kerchiefs around their faces in a vain attempt to keep some of the smell out of their noses.

After an hour of working in silence, Eloise tucked her shovel under her arm and signed, *Why are you acting so weird?*

Johanna jabbed her shovel into the mound of goanna scat so it stood upright. *I'm not acting weird. You're being whiny.*

Whiny? Really?

Johanna grabbed her shovel and threw another shovel load of the scat into the fertilizer slurry. *Really.*

Eloise tossed in two more shovels full.

Johanna did another three.

There. That's what I'm talking about, signed Eloise. *You are competing with me on scat-shoveling.*

I'm not competing. I'm just trying to do a good job. Four more shoveled mounds flew into the slurry vat.

Seriously, Jo. What's up? Yesterday you were competing with me on leech-coddling at the barber's. The day before that it was pot-scrubbing in the kitchens. The day before it was slime-straining from the moat, which followed tomb-dusting in the crypt. That's all after the wood-stacking thing. What the [indistinct gesture] *is going on?*

The two girls matched each other shovel for shovel while Eloise gave Johanna time to respond. She didn't. When it was time to add more water and stir the slurry, they did this in tense silence, too. Eloise accidentally knocked Johanna's paddle as she stirred, and her sister shot her a dirty look. When it happened again, Johanna whacked Eloise's paddle, knocking it out of her hand. The paddle sank to the bottom.

Johanna acted like nothing had happened, while Eloise stood open-mouthed behind her kerchief. *Why did you do that?*

No response.

Eloise took another paddle, poked it in the slurry until she found the sunken one, and scraped it up the side of the vat to where it was almost within reach.

Johanna clunked it again, and it sank back down.

Eloise retaliated by taking a swing at Johanna's paddle. Her sister pulled it away, to protect it, but Eloise's paddle slapped the slurry, sending a plume of it toward her sister. A tiny splash landed on her sleeve.

Disgusted, Johanna retaliated with a splash of her own. Eloise ducked, but a blob caught her on the cheek.

That was it. Whatever this was, it was now war. Eloise raised her paddle, ready to send an almighty wave of the slurry at Johanna, who readied her own paddle in reply.

The melee was fierce. Slurry flew everywhere, and within a minute, both girls were livid and dripping, and much of the slurry was all over the ground.

A cough from the side of the yard pulled them up. "Is there a problem, princesses?" It was Master Hërbërt, rolling a ball of one of his fertilizer combinations toward them, his toothed legs deftly managing the ball, which was bigger than him. Eloise immediately felt foolish. Foolish and disgusting, as slurry dribbled into puddles at her feet.

"That mix that you are disrespecting is crucial to the success of a radish crop near Lower Glenth. I see no reason that the good people of Lower Glenth should suffer due to whatever disagreement appears to be taking place. Do you? Do you have a compelling reason for them to be disadvantaged?"

Eloise shook her head, mortified. Johanna wiped her face on her sleeve and went back to stirring.

"So the next question must be one of recompense."

Both girls looked at him, not understanding.

Master Hërbërt leaned against his fertilizer ball, crossed his top two legs and his bottom two, leaving the middle pair free for gesturing. "Yes, recompense. How will you make good your debt to the people of Lower Glenth? How will you make right this injury they have suffered at your hands?"

This struck Eloise as an awfully crooked line for him to be drawing. To connect the fertilizer slurry splashing to harm done to people living a hundred strong lengths away seemed ludicrous. Or churlish. Or spiteful. Besides, she could barely bring herself to eat radishes.

Then it dawned on Eloise that it might also be true. If the people of Lower Glenth depended on this foul slurry—if it was, as Master Hërbërt said, crucial to their radish success—then Eloise's wasteful actions might, indeed, have a direct impact. Here in the fertilizer yard, the supply of goanna, bat, and lemur scat seemed infinite. But that was impossible, of course. If the Lower Glenthians received less than they needed because she and Johanna were having some sort of spat that she still did not understand—well, that would not do.

Eloise found the slate that Märgärët had left for them, wrote in a very small hand, and held it up for him.

"I'm so sorry, Master Hërbërt de Dung Beetle," he read out loud. "Please forgive my unthinking actions. Would it be OK if I tried to make it up to the good people of Lower Glenth by working an extra shift here in your fertilizer yard after my lessons today? I will pay particular care to the Lower Glenthian radish slurry vat."

He angled his head, considering. "I accept that your words are genuine, and on behalf of the people of Lower Glenth, I accept your offer. You may wash up in that trough."

Johanna snatched the slate and chalk from Eloise, and moments later, had her own message for him. *Master Hërbërt de Dung Beetle. I, too, am sorry for my actions, provoked though they were. I shall work two extra shifts.*

When Eloise read this, she snatched the slate back. *I shall work three extra shifts.*

Johanna held up four fingers, and pointed at herself.

Master Hërbërt shook his head. "You two need to work out your issues. Please do so before you return to my fertilizer yard. I shall, on behalf of the people of Lower Glenth, accept one additional shift from each of you, but not at the same time. That appears to generate too much heat. My fertilizers can't take that."

He rolled his fertilizer ball to where he was making a pyramid of similar ones, positioned it on top, then left the girls cleaning up and stirring the slurry vat.

This is your fault, signed Johanna.

Of course it is, replied Eloise. *It always is.* [Indistinct gesture] *you.*

[Similar indistinct gesture] *you too*.

They'd argued before over the years. Siblings do. But this was different. Very different. It made Eloise sad and angry at the same time. She decided it might be best not to talk to her sister for a while. She'd be polite if spoken to, but she wouldn't initiate any conversation. Apparently Johanna had stuff going on. Best give her space.

20

AT THE BOTTOM OF THE STAIRS

With the ceremony just three days away, the Thorning Master rode them even harder. There was the usual staring at the torture rings, but even more time was spent working with the set of practice thorns. The baroness insisted they must be able to identify the thorns by feel and know their characteristics by heart. The twins (and Märgärët, always Märgärët) worked on trying the different thorns at the various target spots, and experimenting with the way they reacted to them. Eloise still had trouble breaking her skin, but pushed ahead, doing the best she could. Märgärët had no problem thorning herself, as they'd seen from the first day, and Johanna had tried each thorn at least once, even the Çalaht's knitter.

Eloise's aversion to the thorns was at least as strong as her hatred of the needles, and it took an act of will to even handle the things. The deadman's bush, with its numbing, was the only one she could reliably place. The barking vine lotus was also not so bad if she triggered a release from it before it bit in too deeply. The dervish elder spinner, choke lily, thorny olive, and firethorn were harder, as the dizziness, itching, craving for olives, and burning heat seemed to affect her more than the others. The Çalaht's knitter scared her too much to try because of the barb, and the baroness still would not let them try the mad monk's breakfast, as it its effect and their reactions to it were supposed to be a revelation at the end of the ceremony.

Objectively, Eloise thought she was doing a horrible job of preparing, and had no idea how she'd be ready in two days' time.

As the afternoon wore on, she went from one thorn to the next, trying without success to do what was required. "Stop pedaling in the sauer-kraut, and just do it," said the baroness. But no matter how she hovered, hectored, corrected, questioned, and even once or twice encouraged, Eloise got nowhere.

Frustrated, Eloise allowed herself an overdramatic sigh, but the baroness would not have it. "Do not come the offended eggplant with me. Do you think I do this for my health? Trust me, you do not want to be experiencing these thorns for the first time when you are sitting at the dais in front of Court and Çalaht. It will not be easier then, so I suggest you get to where you can do it now."

But Eloise couldn't. She just couldn't. Not with all of them. Not with the depth and ease that the ceremony seemed to demand. When Eloise could not get herself to push a firethorn into the palm of her hand, the baroness gave a guttural noise of disgust, grabbed her cane and headed for the stairs and the long tock, tock, tock of the cane's descent.

Eventually, Eloise noticed there was no "Dismissed!" from below. They were used to the long wait while the baroness climbed down the stairs, but this seemed longer than usual. Much longer.

A shout came from below. "Someone! Help! She's, she's..."

Märgärët leapt up and dashed toward the doorway. Eloise and Johanna followed, bounding down the circular stairs two at a time.

The Thorning Master lay as if she had fallen the last few steps. Her cane had clattered to a halt a few lengths away. She was facedown, with her head on the downward slope. A servant boy stared, afraid to do anything.

Märgärët snapped him out of his paralysis. "Fetch a healer! Or the apothecary! Quick! And perhaps a litter to bring her to her chambers. Go!" She then gently slid the old woman the rest of the way down the steps and rolled her over. "She still breathes." Märgärët snatched off her apron, rolled it up, and put it beneath the Thorning Master's head as a cushion against the cold stone floor. Then she sat down next to her, rubbing a hand. "Baroness, help is coming."

Eloise and Johanna joined her at the baroness's side. Eloise tried a motion she hoped conveyed, "Has she done this before?"

Märgärët seemed to understand. "Not like this. I have come upon her somewhat unresponsive sitting in her armchair, but that was more in the way of a daydream. Or sleep. This... this is different."

At Märgärët's urging, the Thorning Master's eyes opened slowly, and she looked around as though she had no idea where she was. Marvel filled her expression, like a child seeing the grandeur of the castle—or in this case, the castle ceiling—for the first time.

Her eyes found Märgärët, and clarity came to her. "I seem to have had a lapse."

"Yes, Baroness. A small one, perhaps."

"Don't hang noodles from my ears, Märgärët. That is beneath you."

"Yes, Baroness. Apologies. It was likely a significant episode." The Thorning Master tried to sit up, but Märgärët placed a gentle hand on her shoulder, keeping her down. "Rest a few moments, ma'am. Then we will get you to your room."

"I fear I will have plenty of time to rest soon enough. Did I land on my head?"

"Possibly, yes," said Märgärët. "It would appear you fell down the steps."

"I don't remember. My head throbs. Märgärët, I think it may be time."

"Respectfully, Baroness, I don't think so."

"Unfortunately, that is not for you to say. Or me. Çalaht might have some input." Baroness Stúüùbenhocker turned her head left, seeing Eloise. "Hmmm..." Then she turned her head right, where Johanna sat next to Märgärët. "You, young lady."

Johanna nodded and gently grasped the old woman's arm.

"I think you will be fine." With a shaking hand, she reached up and pulled a thorn from her neck. It was a firethorn. "This one may have lost its zing a decade or two ago. Yet, I encourage you to contemplate it. Consider what it means, for you and for your life."

Johanna nodded, eyes tearing. She mouthed a silent, "Thank you," and bowed as best she could while sitting down.

The old woman turned back to Eloise. "You... I don't know about you. But..." With trembling hands, she reached up to her left eye. From it she pulled out the long, purple thorn—the one that Eloise had most fixated on when she first met the baroness. It was not one of the eight that made up the Thorning Ceremony. With a trembling hand, she extended it toward Eloise. "Take it, child. You do not need to practice with it, but consider what it means to have such a thing as part of you." The baroness coughed. "Do not embarrass yourself at the Thorning Ceremony. It would not..." More coughing interrupted her, then subsided. "It would not be becoming for you to have a ceremony like..." She coughed again, ending with a wheeze. "A ceremony like your mother's."

Eloise took the thorn from the Thorning Master. She put her palms together and bowed a silent thank you.

"Märgärët! Are you there?" said the Baroness.

"Yes, ma'am. Right here. Let me get you to your room so we can have you tended."

The ancient woman used some of her fading strength to wave that off. "I have something for you as well." For the third time, she used her trembling hand, first removing a ring, and then reaching to her crown to retrieve something hidden in her hair. It was a needle-sharp thorn from a mad monk's breakfast, except it was cast in silver so polished that it glinted in the light from a nearby window. She handed both to Märgärët. "Märgärët von den Kleiderschrankbenutzer, I thank you for your service and your companionship. Please take these and perhaps think upon me from time to time."

"No, Baroness. Please. You're not going anywhere. Nothing is going on that a strong haggleberry tea and some of your favorite shortbread biscuits won't fix." The tears streaming down her face made a lie of her words.

"Don't comb the giraffe, Märggïïëë. There's not time."

"Please, don't leave me. Don't leave me alone. I'm not ready. Not ready at all."

"We knew this day was coming. Well, here it is."

Running feet and calling voices neared them. Careful, efficient hands lifted the Thorning Master onto a canvas stretcher, and two guards hefted it to take her to her rooms.

"It reveals," muttered the old woman to Märgärët. "The Thorning Ceremony—it reveals about the Thorning Master as well. Mind that."

Those were the last words Eloise ever heard from Baroness Stúüùben-hocker. By the morning, she had exhaled her last breath and her spirit had flown. The queen had arranged that the baroness's deathbed be attended by a healer, an endwife, and, briefly, the Venerated Prelate Herself. Märgärët, of course, was there to the end, and it was she who, sleepless, red-eyed, and in shock, conveyed the news to the twins in the Seclusion Room with a simple, "She is gone." Then she left them in the room, door ajar, with no instructions.

Eloise was saddened, but not too, too much. She briefly wondered whether the baroness would be allowed to stand with Çalaht in the afterlife. She assumed so. The Thorning Master had lived what appeared to have been an upright life. It would have been interesting to be a fly on the Holy One's wall when she made her divine pronouncement upon the old woman's soul, if for no other reason than to see how that process worked.

If Eloise was honest, though, what she felt most of all was relief. Relief that without a Thorning Master, there could be no Thorning Ceremony. That was something she could live with.

21

THE BAGEL EMBROIDERER

Eloise had not seen her mother, other than at a distance and in passing, since giving herself over to Baroness Stúúüben-hocker. With the Thorning Master's passing, she was not surprised that she and Johanna had been summoned. Eloise wondered if the queen would postpone the Thorning Ceremony, or (and this was Eloise's preference), cancel it altogether. Time would tell.

Earlier, she had tried to ask Johanna through sign language if she thought the rules were still in effect, but her sister didn't seem to want to talk. So Eloise kept quiet on her side of the Seclusion Room and thought about when she might be allowed to eat something that wasn't miso soup.

Then came the herald with the summons from the queen. To Eloise's surprise, they'd been called to the Declaiming Room, and not the Receiving Room, or even their private Salle de la Famille, where these sorts of things were usually handled. There was nothing to declaim, except maybe the old woman's passing. So what was the point of using the Declaiming Room?

They arrived to find their mother sitting on her throne, illuminated by a hard mid-morning light that glared off the room's marble floor and walls. She spoke quietly to a group of two dozen Court hangers-on dressed in black, including several porcupines and echidnas. The inevitable scribe scratched the proceedings onto hemp parchment.

The warm brightness of the room was incongruous with the overall mood of the people. Queen Eloise II wore a simple robe of ebony and gray, her hair was tied in a mourner's plait, and she wore a silver, elongated thumb as a sop to the strict Çalahtists who hung around Court and made snotty comments if she didn't. On her lap was the Declaiming Robe, which she embroidered. The robe was a heavy, out-of-style number in faded purple with boofy sleeves and decorative stitching that was added to by each successive queen, the stitching depicting their predecessor in some way (not always flattering). The line of queens definitely had variable skills with needle and thread. Queen Eloise, for example, embroidered out of obligation, not skill or love, and appeared to be stitching a bagel onto it. The Declaiming Robe had been worn by Gumballs for centuries, and was steeped in tradition, history, and a musty smell that just would not wash out.

The queen waved her daughters over, indicating that they should stand in front of her, not sit beside her as Eloise would have expected.

Something was up.

"Girls, thank you for coming."

Eloise wanted to respond, "Like we had a choice," but she kept silent, because that was what Johanna was doing. Best to err on the side of caution. Plus, the queen did not seem to be in a mood where snark would be appreciated.

"It is very sad to lose someone as beloved as the Thorning Master." The queen said this with a straight face, although it had been obvious from even before the old woman first shuffle-shuffle-tock-paused into the Receiving Room that Baroness Stúüübenhocker would never be first on the queen's Yule card list. "Our departed Thorning Master served all the realms admirably and with dedication, a service that spanned generations. Both my mother and grandmother had naught but praise for her, and it is with sadness and appreciation that we remember her, and pray that she now stands with Çalaht."

The hangers on gave a quiet, "Hear, hear," and Eloise could have sworn she heard one of the porcupines sniffing back tears.

"Her untimely passing presents..." The queen seemed to imitate the baroness by letting a silence hang for way too long. "It presents difficulties. Girls, I apologize, but I'll need to postpone the ceremony."

Eloise could not help but grin in relief. She bowed her head and stared at her clunky servant's shoes, trying to hide her smile.

"Instead of it taking place in two days, it shall take place in three."

Eloise's smile cratered. That was hardly a delay at all. It wouldn't make any difference to her ability (or lack thereof) to get through the ceremony. She was glad she was looking downward, or the queen would have seen the change in her expression.

Perhaps her mother intended to be Thorning Master and lead the ceremony. She was queen, so she could if she wanted. Eloise didn't think that would be an improvement on the late baroness.

"You may step back."

The queen tied off the thread on her half-finished bagel and snipped the remaining thread free. The girls moved toward the back of the dais and watched the queen stand and put on the Declaiming Robe.

"I call before me Märgärët von den Kleiderschrankbenutzer."

Eloise had not seen the servant standing at the back of the room. She no longer wore servant's clothes. Instead, she was dressed in an elegant, simple mourner's gown, and a black lace widow's veil. Red eyes betrayed recent tears, but they were dry and focused now. She stepped forward to the dais.

"Märgärët von den Kleiderschrankbenutzer, I would offer you the role of Thorning Master to the Western Lands and All That Really Matters. Would you be willing to serve our realm in this way?"

There was a pause where only the scratch of the scribe's quill could be heard. Märgärët blinked back tears and swallowed. "Yes, Queen Eloise. I would."

"Will you conduct your office with all the skill and knowledge you can bring to bear upon it?"

Another slight hesitation, then, "Yes, Queen Eloise, I will."

"Will you be ready to conduct your first Thorning Ceremony for Princess Eloise and Princess Johanna in three days?"

Eloise saw uncertainty steal over Märgärët's face. "Yes. Yes, I believe I will be. That should be enough time for me to prepare."

"Good enough. Märgärët von den Kleiderschrankbenutzer, I do hereby proclaim you Thorning Master. I grant you all appropriate titles and claims upon lands and privileges in my realm that accrue to this role. Being Thorning Master to the Western Lands and All That Really Matters will help you pursue the title in the other three and a half realms, although it's not like you'll have a lot of competition."

"Thank you, Queen Eloise."

"May Çalaht guide you in your duties, and may her gap-toothed smile rain blessings down upon you."

"Thank you, Queen Eloise. I shall serve at your pleasure, and if Çalaht wills it, at the pleasure of the other monarchs. May I ask you to please witness my first thorning in this role?"

The queen's face twitched. "Yes, of course."

Märgärët removed a cloth from her pocket and unwrapped the silver mad monk's breakfast thorn that the baroness had given to her the day before. It had been polished, and glinted even more than it had before in the mid-morning light. The new Thorning Master lifted her widow's veil to expose her face, pinched a flap of skin at her left temple, and pushed the silver thorn completely through it.

Eloise had spent weeks watching the baroness, Märgärët, and even Johanna doing this kind of thing, so watched unfazed. The hangers-on, however, were completely unprepared. They gasped, winced, and one or two seemed to stifle a gag.

"Thank you, Queen Eloise. Honor to the Queen."

"Honor to the Thorning Master."

"May I address the princesses?"

"Yes."

Märgärët flipped down the widow's veil and walked over to the girls. Two trickles of blood dribbled from the piercings where the silver thorn stuck out. "Princess Eloise. Princess Johanna." Her voice was an exhausted whisper, and when she knew she had their attention, she dropped eye contact. "The late baroness taught you as best she could. Now it is up to you to use what you've learned. I will need the full time available to prepare, so will not see you before the Thorning Ceremony. I ask you to maintain your silence, but I hereby lift the other restrictions. You may go about the castle as you please, but I suggest you return to your rooms and spend the time readying yourselves. Gather yourselves well. I will see you when the ceremony starts at dusk three days hence. Understood?"

They nodded.

With a final curtsy to the queen, Märgärët left the Declaiming Room.

When the queen dismissed the twins, Eloise walked out of the room feeling both elation at her restored freedoms and dread at the prospect of having only three days to overcome her inabilities with the thorns.

22

ANTSY

With nothing better to do, Eloise headed for her room.

Her own room. Bliss. She couldn't wait to shut the door, and lay on her very own bed. She might never leave the room again. Well, maybe to visit Jerome now and then, and get food. But that was all. If the past weeks had taught her anything, it was that going about the castle and doing everything that needed doing was vastly overrated.

She turned the last corner and stopped. Her door was ajar. Someone was in there. All she wanted was peace and quiet, a chance for solitude, but no. She was going to have to deal with someone.

She crept forward so she could peek in.

It was the quince jam servant girl. The aardvark. Shame flushed Eloise's cheeks at the memory of their last encounter. Eloise really did not want to interact with this particular servant again. At least she had a slate this time, and could tell explain that she didn't want her tongue cut out.

Eloise considered going somewhere else. Anywhere else. Maybe the Salle des Champions. It was usually quiet there. Or she could find an empty corner in the Hall of Bald Opulence —unless they were already preparing the room for the ceremony. There were plenty of places to hide in the castle, it was just that none of them were her room. After all those weeks in the Seclusion Room, she was desperate for her own space.

No. No more embarrassment. She would deal with this head on. Eloise stepped up to the threshold and waved

The aardvark didn't see her and continued dusting the fireplace mantel. Eloise had a new appreciation for dusting since their tomb-dusting morning in the crypt. She also had a much better sense of what it took to get fresh sheets onto her bed, clean clothes on her back, and the fires burning for her food. Eloise could see that the servant was being very careful to pick up the objects on the mantel, swoosh her duster and then, with great precision, put them back exactly as they had been. Eloise (and her habits, which liked things to be in their place) appreciated this care.

Eloise knocked twice on the door frame to let the aardvark know she was there, and smiled what she hoped was a very friendly smile. The servant turned, gasped, and instinctively clapped a hand over her mouth to protect her tongue. Then she curtsied and started backing away. "Princess Eloise. I didn't know you were there. I'm sorry. I'm so, so sorry. Please don't—"

Eloise held up a hand, stopping her. She took her slate and a piece of chalk from her pocket and wrote, *Hello, Läääcy. How are you today? Thank you for cleaning my room.* She held it up for the servant to read.

The aardvark stepped forward, looked at the slate, and shook her head. "You've written words. I don't have my letters yet."

Well, that was inconvenient. And something that ought to be fixed. How was Eloise supposed to get anything across?

Then, unexpectedly, the servant smiled at Eloise. A huge smile. "I don't have my letters, but I know the shape of my name. You've remembered my name! That's the first time you got my name right on the first try. Thank you, Princess."

Eloise smiled and mouthed a mute "You're welcome." She then motioned around, indicating the room, then pressed her palms together and bowed a thank you to Läääcy.

The aardvark's eyes went wide. The shock of Eloise's gesture flummoxed her. Reflexively, she pressed her paws together and returned the gesture.

So Eloise did it again. Läääcy repeated her response, leading Eloise to do it again, and Läääcy to do the same. They went back and forth like this until they both started giggling. At last, they performed the gesture simultaneously, and then stopped.

They stood there looking at each other, smiling. Eloise was confident that Läääcy no longer felt her tongue was in danger.

Läääcy curtsied again as a servant would, and said, "I'm done in your room. The sheets are clean, and your clothes are away in your trunk, just the way you like them. Can I bring you anything from the kitchen?"

Eloise erased the slate and did her best to draw a teapot and a scone.

"Tea and a vol-au-vent. I'll fetch them for you now." Läääcy slipped out the door and headed for the kitchens.

Eloise really needed to do something about her drawing skills.

Her first inclination was to strip down, crawl into bed, and lose herself in sleep. But then she'd end up having her tea and vol-au-vent feeling all groggy. That wouldn't do. She paced around her room, reacquainting herself with its contents, picking things up and placing them down, making the slightest adjustments to suit her habits. Seeing her things again also reminded her that she'd have to go get her personal items from the Seclusion Room. Her comb would soon be back with its twin and the hairbrush. Soon, all would be right again.

Except, of course, it wouldn't. Three days from now she was going to embarrass herself in front of friends, family, and Court. If Eloise had learned anything about herself, it was that there was nothing in all the four-and-a-half realms that would get her through the Thorning Ceremony. Eloise didn't think it would make a difference if Çalaht herself appeared and tried to help her out. Her pain threshold was just too low, and her propensity to faint was just too high. Johanna seemed to have worked it out. Märgärët obviously managed it—she was good enough to be made Thorning Master. Eloise just had to be prepared to wear the shame.

How did people get through the ceremony? Her mother, for example. Her mother got through it. She wouldn't talk about it, but she'd managed it. The baroness had said that her mother's Thorning Ceremony revealed "control, determination, and a certain coldness." That sure sounded like the queen.

Something niggled at her—something else the baroness had said. What was it? It was something like, "Your mother's Thorning Ceremony. Well, that's a matter of public record, a record that I'm sure has found its way to an unlikely box or corner somewhere."

The baroness implied that it was something her mother would not want discovered. That meant it was absolutely something that Eloise should find.

Eloise grabbed a quill and parchment, just in case she needed to make notes. As she walked out the door, she was stopped by Läääcy coming in holding a tray.

"Are you no longer hungry, Princess?" asked the servant. "I brought tea. It took me a while to find a vol-au-vent, but..." She fished something out of her pocket and set it on the tray. "I also snuck a couple of these gibbous moon biscuits when Chef wasn't looking, although I suspect she was not looking very hard on purpose."

Eloise mouthed, "Thank you," then put a biscuit in her apron pocket, pointed to herself, mimed two fingers walking, pointed to the quill and parchment, mimed reading something and taking notes, pointed at a biscuit, pointed at the servant, pointed at the tea, pointed again at the servant, mimed sipping and nibbling, and then mimed an exaggerated smile and a belch. She had no expectation at all that Läääcy would understand.

"Oh, Princess, that's very kind of you. I'd love a biscuit, and I'll take one for later. But I'll pass on the tea for now, as I have much to do today. Enjoy your time in the Bibliotheca de Records and Regrets. If you need anything when you get back, please just let me know." She bowed, spun around, and took the tray back to the kitchens.

Eloise had made herself understood. That was a nice surprise.

She headed for the Bibliotheca. There was a secret to discover.

❧ 23 ❧

BIBLIOTHECA DE RECORDS
AND REGRETS

Eloise found Master Overbolt asleep in their study nook in the Bibliotheca de Records and Regrets. As always at this time of day, he was slumped down in his chair, which tilted back against the stone wall on two legs. His mouth gaped, his snoring rattled, and saliva dripped like a metronome onto his tunic. She considered how she might wake him without him being annoyed at being caught. Drop a scroll? Knock? No, too likely to generate ire.

Then she saw his quill. Eloise grabbed it, lightly tickled one of his golden ear tufts until he reacted just a little, then ducked behind her *Livre de Protocol* as if she was studying.

Overbolt's chair jolted down on the stone floor. "Weasels," he exclaimed in his squeaky voice. "Parsnips, hoosegow, wabbit, dotard, antithetical!" He rubbed the top of his head. When he saw Eloise, he dropped his hand, assuming a lesson must be in progress. "I'm sorry. Can you repeat the question?"

Eloise showed him what she'd written on her slate. *Good Master Overbolt. Where might I find the records for the Thorning Ceremonies over the years?*

"The Thorning Ceremony records? Hmmm... Not much call for those. Mind, I can understand why you might be curious." He tried to covertly rub spittle from the corner of his mouth, and brushed at the damp spot on his tunic. "Head Scribe would know. We could ask him."

Eloise wrote. *He's busy, I think, with the Queen. Saw him on my way here.* This was a lie of convenience, but she doubted Master Overbolt would try to corroborate it.

"Not to worry. It will no doubt be in the Scroll of Scrolls."

The Scroll of Scrolls was supposed to list everything in the Bibliotheca de Records and Regrets and where it was found. As far as Eloise could tell, the massive scroll did exactly that. The problem was, there was no order to it. It was simply a chronological-ish, somewhat topically clustered listing of all the scrolls that came in, which meant finding a particular listing was somewhere between exceptionally challenging and completely impossible.

Who did the looking was as important as where they looked. Head Scribe knew much of the Scroll of Scrolls off by heart, so asking him was faster than actually scanning through it. Master Overbolt was less familiar, but tenacious in his own way. More than once, Eloise had overheard him tell someone, "No, no. I'll keep looking. Now it's personal." Usually, he succeeded.

Eloise followed her tutor out of the study nook and through aisles of dusty shelves, until they reached a massive scroll just inside the front vestibule. It was easily three times the size of her study copy of the *Livre de Protocol*, and was scrolled one third of the way through. A quick glance showed that the last person to use it must have been researching northeast sector oat harvests from the previous century. That, or leopard education initiatives instigated under Queen Yvonne Octave Barbell Gumball II.

For almost an hour, Eloise watched Master Overbolt scroll forward and backward through the Scroll of Scrolls, muttering the names of different scroll clusters. "Wombat burrow reclamation projects," he said, half to himself and half to her. "Elbow and hock census collection, principles thereof. Proceedings of the Third Annual Flax-Adjacent Guilds Conclave. Fava Bean Soup Recipes. Something to do with competitive toffee stretching, but it's obscured by a toffee stain. Rope production statistics, a comparison of those for the Half Kingdom and the Eastern Lands. An analysis of Queen Gwendolyn's use of the term 'pillock.' Royal visits. Royal rows. Royal stormings off in huffs..." The random listing of scrolls careened from the mundane to the absurd and back.

Somewhere around "Fibrous Plant Reporting Requirements," Eloise nodded off, only to be awakened with a sharp, "Aha!"

Find something? she wrote.

"Sadly, no. It is a set of scrolls that document the use of the term 'Aha' by inventors. There's a similar set of scrolls that elaborate the use of 'Oh, never mind.' And look, they're right next to each other on the shelves. Curious, that."

Eloise knew she had to give him the time he needed, and after another half hour, her patience was rewarded. "Here we are, Princess. There's a listing here for a set of scrolls that cover, and I quote, 'Ceremonies and Suchlike, Royal, Pertaining To or Involving Various Objects, Pointy.' You would consider the Thorning Ceremony as involving various pointy objects, would you not?"

Yes, Master Overbolt. I'd say so.

"Then that's our destination. Sixth level. Top floor. Bin 185, sub-bin 422, sub-sub-bin A7, sub-sub-sub-bin Mabel. Please follow me."

❧ 24 ❧

SUB-SUB-SUB-BIN MABEL

E loise had never been that high in the Bibliotheca before, and judging from the way Master Overbolt wheezed his bulk upward from step to step, he did not get up there very often either. His face and tunic were soaked by floor four, and Eloise worried she'd have to go fetch a healer, or maybe an endwife, by the time they reached the top. To her relief, Master Overbolt proved equal to the task, if only just.

He waved for her to follow, then lumbered into the room full of shelves and scroll stacks. Bin 185, sub-bin 422, sub-sub-bin A7, sub-sub-sub-bin Mabel was inconveniently located at the back of the hallway, but clearly labeled, right between bin 185, sub-bin 422, sub-sub-bin A7, sub-sub-sub-bin Larry, "Ceremonies and Suchlike, Royal, Pertaining To or Involving Various Objects, Sharp" and bin 185, sub-bin 422, sub-sub-bin A7, sub-sub-sub-bin Nelson, "Ceremonies and Suchlike, Royal, Pertaining To or Involving Various Objects, Sticky."

Sub-sub-sub-bins Larry, Mabel, and Nelson all turned out to be the size of royal carriages. They were crammed full of scrolls, some of which looked like they had been there since Çalaht's grime-encrusted feet trod the realms.

Eloise wrote, *Is there an order?* and held it up for Master Overbolt to consider.

"I'm sure there is. There is order in all of Çalaht's natural world. Our role as scholars and theologians is to find it."

So, no.

"Sadly not."

Thank you, Master Overbolt. I'll be as fast as possible.

"Find me on your way out. Otherwise, I'll have to climb back up here to look for you."

Eloise bowed, a combination of "Yes" and "Thank you." She watched her tutor walk away, then turned to face the overwhelming wall of scrolls.

She knew which year she needed to find—the year her mother turned fourteen. She then had to guess what method the scribes and scholars used for deciding where in sub-sub-sub-bin Mabel they went. On top? Closest? Wherever they could reach?

One by one, she took a dozen scrolls out, looking to see what they were about and when they were from. None of them were anywhere close to what she needed, or even the quarter century she sought. Plus, it appeared that "Ceremonies and Suchlike, Royal, Pertaining To or Involving Various Objects, Pointy" covered all kinds of weird stuff, some of which Eloise had heard of, and some of which she was sure would never have found their way into the *Livre de Protocol*, or even polite society.

There was a dusty scroll from a century past that was A Treatise on the Ceremonial Removal By the Use of Picks of Objects Accidentally Frozen in Ice. Several scrolls covered speeches used to open the Festival of Forks and Sporks held every year at Flatware Flats. There was a scroll recording "The Blessing of the Prickly Pears by Gáäävin the Optimist at Gáäävin's Cove," next to one that was from the following year describing "The Banishment of Prickly Pears by Gáäävin the Surprised at Gáäävin's Cove." A third, from the year after that, covered "The Burning of Prickly Pears by Gááàvin the Desperate at Gááàvin's Cove," and a fourth gave an account of "The Abandonment of Gááàvin's Cove by Gááàvin the Resigned."

There was nothing to do but just dive in and try to find the thing. For the next two hours, Eloise pulled out, dusted off, de-cobwebbed, examined, and replaced hundreds of scrolls from sub-sub-sub-bin Mabel. She would have loved to have spent more time reading about "The Queen's Inspection Techniques for the Control of Awl Quality" or "The Noblewoman's Guide to Divining Weather Through the Interpretation of Dropped Pins," but she had to stay focused. She searched past "Proper Prod Placement When in Military Processions," an "Account of an Attack Against a Taxman's Tack Tax," and "Innovative Costumery Based on the Donation of Stingers from Bees and Wasps."

She resisted the temptations of "The Use of, and Subsequent Dedications for, Spiked Inclines in Castle Gardens," an essay on "The Benedictions of Pikes, and the Unexpected Dangers of Incessantly Humming Annoying Tunes Around Pikemen," "An Exegesis on the Use of Pointed Remarks by Minor Nobles" (probably misfiled), "A Complete and Accurate Guide to Addresses Made Before the Secret Society for Surreptitiously Promoting Dental Hygiene, Toothpick Division," and "Royal Proclamations Concerning Various and Sundry Vegetables That Can Be Successfully Deployed for Shish Kebab Celebration and Praise."

All raised some degree of curiosity in Eloise, but all were off topic. She found a List of Thorny Words (also probably misfiled), but that was as close as she got to her goal. Sub-sub-sub-bin Mabel's scrolls yielded no records of Thorning Ceremonies. At least not in the places where she had looked.

Even if she did find a set of scrolls recording Thorning Ceremonies, would a record of her mother's ceremony have been properly stored with them? If it existed at all, it could be anywhere. The baroness had suggested it had probably found its way to "an unlikely box or corner somewhere," so was sub-sub-sub-bin Mabel even the right place to look?

No, Eloise couldn't think like that. She had to work under the assumption that it was here, and that it was worth finding. Surely, that was worth a few more hours of her time.

Eloise looked at sub-sub-sub-bin Mabel. She had to think like a scribe or a scholar. If she was trying to hide something, where would she put it? Scribes and scholars were all about knowledge. They collected it, learned it, savored it, dropped it, but most of all, they respected it. It would go against the grain for a scholar to remove knowledge from circulation, never to be seen again. So, how do you hide something without hiding it, or without making it possible for someone else to eventually find it if it was really, really needed?

Put it underneath? Climb up and shove it down the back? If the scholars and scribes were anything like Master Overbolt (and most of them were), the odds of them climbing anywhere were pretty low. It would have been a matter of placing, not clambering.

She took a few steps back to reconsider sub-sub-sub-bin Mabel. While she was at it, she looked at Larry and Nelson as well. Sharp, pointy, sticky. Sharp, pointy, sticky.

The path of least resistance would be to simply misfile them nearby and leave a clue pointing to their whereabouts. She'd have to find it quickly—the room was losing light as the sun moved toward dusk. She walked over to sub-sub-sub-bin Larry, looking for a clue, but nothing jumped out at her. She did the same with sub-sub-sub-bin Nelson, scanning the frame that held the scrolls. Again, nothing.

Except...

In the lower right-hand corner, it looked like someone had scrawled something. A question mark showed through a layer of dust and cobwebs. Eloise used her elbow to wipe the spot clean. It read "Something missing? Look behind you."

Eloise spun around. On the opposite side of the aisle was bin 183, sub-bin 896, sub-sub-bin E14, sub-sub-sub-bin Alphonso, "Religious Records Re. Reliquarium Rituals, Pertaining To or Involving Various Prayers, Blasphemous."

She walked over to Alphonso and considered it. The sub-sub-sub-bin was bigger than Larry, Mabel, and Nelson put together. There was no way she'd find anything just looking randomly. Using the cuff of her sleeve, she wiped down the edges of the frame, looking for another clue.

Then she saw it—an asterisk drawn on a hard-to-reach part of Alphonso. Eloise saw that the dust layer on the scrolls was different— less ancient than the dust on its neighbors. She pulled out a scroll from the middle. "Being a Record of the Thorning Ceremony of Joan Mendacity Penultimate Gumball." Eloise recognized Queen Joan the Sadly Befuddled from her portrait in the Salon des Champions, as well as from Histories and Hearsay lessons.

She'd found the records.

❧ 25 ❧
TWO DISASTERS AND A
SUCCESS

E loise unrolled Queen Joan's scroll (she was recorded as
Princess Joan in it) to see what was there. A date, a record of
those in attendance (around a dozen dozen), and an account
of the proceedings. The scribe had, as the baroness said, recorded the
placement of the thorns as well as the timing. Young Joan had chosen a
firethorn in the wisdom eye, a dervish elder spinner at her throat, and
the choke lilies and mad monk's breakfasts in her neck. Most of those
seemed like reasonable choices. The notes said that the ceremony
went "apace" and "finished reasonably." The mad monk's breakfasts
induced a "state of dumbstruck curiosity" and a "sudden desire for
items upon which the princess might 'munch.'"

Interesting.

The scroll also noted the tone of Court gossip, which sniped about her
choice of dress, but was otherwise generally favorable.

Eloise unfurled a second scroll, this one for Princess Yvonne Octave
Barbell Gumball IV, another name she recognized. This document was
scribed quite differently than the first. There was the same title and
date, but instead of paragraphs of text, the scribe had rendered a beau-

tiful, if nightmarish, drawing of the princess. In simple quill strokes, he captured the girl's agony, thorns protruding in lifelike detail, droplets of blood accenting her pain. The artist had not labeled the thorns, relying instead on the reader's knowledge. There was a Çalaht's knitter hooked through her hand, and the strange stringy hooks of the barking vine lotus dangling from her temples. Tears streaked the princess's face and she looked like she might pass away from the pain. The scribe had even captured the sense of thirst caused by the thorny olives.

Not a drawing to keep in one's sleeping chamber.

There were only a few words. "Adequate, if disappointing." "Slow and unimaginative." Eloise thought those words were a fair description of the reign of Queen Yvonne Octave Barbell Gumball IV.

It was like the baroness had said—the Thorning Ceremony reveals.

Eloise rifled through the scrolls. She could tell by the color of the hemp parchment and the thickness of the dust which newer. She looked for these, ignoring the chance (for now, at least) to learn something of her forebears.

It took another quarter hour. Someone had definitely made it difficult to find the scroll, sliding it into one from 160 years before, and tucking it at the bottom of the cluster of Thorning Ceremony records, but Eloise found it. The hemp parchment was still a bleached white, not yellowed with age. To her surprise, Eloise even recognized the scribe's handwriting. It was the Head Scribe's hand that had written, "Being a Record of the Thorning Ceremonies of Eloise Hydra Gumball II."

Ceremonies? Plural? Odd.

There were three leaves of parchment scrolled together. Three different dates. Three different ceremonies.

The first was short. "The Thorning Master began the Thorning Ceremony as expected in the Throne Hall. However, during the initial words by the Venerated Prelate Herself, Princess Eloise Hydra Gumball II appeared exceptionally nervous, and when the time came to place the first thorn, was unable to complete the task due to a sudden reappearance of both her lunch and breakfast. She departed the Hall of Bald Opulence posthaste and did not return during the day. The gateaux and fig bars prepared in celebration were nonetheless served. (Chef is my hero.)" There was also a note that said, "The Thorning Master appeared displeased."

It was hard for Eloise to picture. She'd seen a portrait of her mother from around that time. Even then, she had looked in control, a bit aloof, and as though she would tolerate no nonsense. It seemed impossible that she'd lost control of her stomach and run out of the room, forcing the postponement of the ceremony.

Eloise turned to the second page. The dates showed that they'd tried again the next day, this time in the smaller Hall of Authority. The result was not much better. Her mother had made it through the Venerated Prelate Herself's benediction, and the recorded words were the usual dull, overly religious Çalahtist hooey that Venerable Prelates Themselves were prone to. Eloise wondered if it had been the same tapir who served now, or her predecessor who, if Eloise wasn't mistaken, had been a vole.

The Thorning Master began, with Queen Eloise the First leading those gathered in drumming, which was supposed to help induce a trance state. The scribe summarized the next bit as, "Princess Eloise Hydra Gumball II began the placing of thorns with the deadman's bush in the crown of her head, changed her mind, put the firethorn there, changed her mind, attempted to put the Çalaht's knitter there, was unable to, placed the thorny olive, went back to the firethorn, replaced it with the choke lily, replaced this with the dervish elder, went back to the firethorn, then used the mad monk's breakfast, which induced uncontrollable sobbing. The drumming faltered, and the process was again abandoned. The shortbread and tortes that were prepared in celebration were served, nonetheless. (Chef is still my hero.)" There was again a final note: "The Thorning Master appeared most displeased."

A second disaster.

Her mother was probably lucky that Eloise's grandmother's marriage was, by then, a festering wound whose open warfare dominated Court gossip. The queen and king's legendary enmity would have diverted a lot of attention from these Thorning Ceremony failures.

The third attempt took place a week later. It was back in the Throne Room. The Venerated Prelate Herself delivered a benediction that was recorded as "mercifully shorter than last time," and the Thorning Master began the ceremony. The scribe noted that "Princess Eloise Hydra Gumball II displayed a self-control and determination fit for a future queen as she placed the thorns flawlessly and with a stoic indifference to whatever discomfiture she might be experiencing."

Well, that was different. Eloise wondered what had changed.

Eloise read through the record of her thorn placement. A Çalaht's knitter in the crown, firethorns in the front of the neck either side of her throat, thorny olives in the back of her neck either side of her spine, a dervish elder spinner in her throat and heart areas, the itchy ones in her hands—the list went on. It did not strike Eloise as particularly inspired, just efficient, direct. The scribe noted that the mad monk's breakfast "Induced a state of grim, glassy-eyed, quiet immobility that lasted an extended time."

The scribe also commented on how delicious the aquafaba meringues and coagulated lemon curdle were, and speculated that perhaps he should propose to Chef.

Eloise sat and repeatedly re-read the three parchment leaves. Her mother, the stoic, in-control, unemotional character who now sat on the throne had had a disaster of a Thorning Ceremony. That explained the awkwardness with the baroness.

The baroness had said her mother's Thorning Ceremony revealed "control, determination, and a certain coldness." Not on the first or second tries, that was for sure. Those were disasters. But it sounded like a fair description of the third. Eloise wondered what the late Old Pincushion had done to whip her mother into shape. A lecture about "Know Your Why?" Stern words? Maybe her methods were different back then, or maybe someone else had helped. Or maybe her mother had just put on her big girl's tunic and gotten on with it. Whatever had happened, it worked. Her mother had made it and had been proclaimed Future Ruler and Heir.

It gave Eloise hope.

Not a solution, but hope.

LIKE SISTERS DO

The morning of the Thorning Ceremony dawned crisp and bright—the exact opposite of how Eloise felt. After discovering just how badly her mother's Thorning Ceremony had gone, Eloise had gone back to her room to confront the parcel of thorns the Thorning Master had given her.

It hadn't gone well.

One by one, Eloise had attempted to place the thorns in the parts of her face, neck, and hands, as she would have to do that afternoon. The deadman's bush was still the only one she could place reliably, due to the numbing effect. Worst was the Çalaht's knitter. The idea of shoving it all the way through to get it out made her want to retch. The others fell in between, with the thorny olive and the choke lily being the only two she could almost tolerate. She had no idea how she'd make it through the ritual.

At least she wasn't still fainting all the time. That was something.

Nerves gathered in the pit of Eloise's stomach. She thought about "Know your why." Intellectually, she got it—the need to prove it to herself. But that understanding still had not reached her gut, and she was running out of time. "There's no way I can do this," became her mantra of despair.

Eloise tried to focus on things she could control, but no amount of combing her hair, counting the cracks in her bedroom floor, or laying out the new, specially made dress could settle her. As sun rose from dawn to morning, she found herself spiraling into a near panic, saying "I can't" over and over.

Johanna. She'd talk to her sister. She, more than anyone, would understand what Eloise was going through. Maybe Johanna would share something that might help, despite the strain between them.

Eloise looked out the window to gage how late it was. Johanna was not a morning person on the best of days, and today was unlikely to be anywhere close to "best." But Eloise was desperate. She'd been up all night, and she guessed that maybe Johanna had been, too. She decided to risk Johanna's morning wrath.

Eloise opened her door to an empty hall, save for the breakfast odors of peach porridge and cinnamon scones. Normally, that would have triggered an immediate chowing down, but Eloise was too far gone with nerves to even consider it. She certainly did not want a performance like her mother's first Thorning Ceremony.

She rapped gently on her sister's closed door using the pattern of knocks that identified her.

Johanna flung open the door. She wore a snow-white morning robe, not her usual pink and lace dressing gown. Half a dozen thorns protruded from Johanna's neck, face and hands. Clearly Johanna was getting in some last-minute practice.

What do you want? she signed.

Can we talk?

Is there anything to say?

Never mind. Johanna's cold hostility was more than Eloise was prepared for. Unbidden, tears fell.

ANDREW EINSPRUCH

Johanna gave an exasperated shrug and waved her sister in. She sat her at her vanity and handed her a clean handkerchief.

Eloise wiped her eyes and blew her nose. Then she pointed to the thorns sticking out of her sister. *How do you do it? What's the secret?*

Secret? There's no secret. It hurts! A lot. The "secret" is that I put up with the pain. Johanna pulled a thorn out from her neck. *You could, too. I think you are being cowardly. You choose not to deal with the pain. That is a coward's way.*

Eloise's jaw dropped. So much for comfort. So much for sisterly help.

[Indistinct gesture] *you!*

Whatever. Johanna turned her back and picked up another thorn—a Çalaht's knitter. Turning, she held it up dramatically for Eloise to see. Then just as dramatically, she dashed it into her hand, driving the hook through.

A perfect thorn placement.

Johanna waggled it at her twin. *See you later. If you make it, that is.*

Eloise fought off wooziness and shouldered her way out of Johanna's room. She closed the door behind her and sagged against it. Coward? Coward! How dare she!

But it was true. She was scared witless. Brave people were scared, but did things anyway. Cowards were scared and faffed around. She was absolutely at the flapping around end of the scale.

But it wasn't too late. Eloise went over to her vanity, where the collection of thorns was laid out. If Johanna could do it, so could she. She picked up a dervish elder spinner, one of the thorns she'd not been able to do yet. Eloise held it up dramatically, showing it to a Johanna who was not there, and jammed it into her wisdom eye. Pain shot through her, combined with the dizziness caused by the spinner.

Eloise fainted.

She lay unconscious for a long time.

❧ 27 ❧

ANCESTORS ALL

The Thorning Ceremony dress that Seamstress Linttrap had sewn was exquisite. The cotton fabric was some of the finest Eloise had ever seen, dyed to a midnight blue. The sleeves and skirt were embroidered with a pattern of vines and trees in black thread. The bodice-style top, laced at the back so that it flattered, was a lighter, complementary blue, brocaded in a pattern of thorns. On any other day, Eloise would have been delighted. Today, she barely noticed it.

Läääcy de Aardvark had found Eloise crumpled on the ground, a knot swelling on the back of her head where she'd clunked it against the floor. The servant had wanted to fetch a healer, or at least the Apothecary, but Eloise had convinced her to just help her get dressed and get her to the Throne Hall on time. Fortunately, her hair hid the bump, which throbbed in time to the race of her pulse.

She made it to her seat in the Hall of Bald Opulence late enough to raise eyebrows, but not so late as to warrant comment. Next to her, Johanna sat straight and still, eyes forward, wearing a matching dress dyed a compatible deep burgundy. She had done up her hair in a simple tight braid that hung down her back and stayed out of the way. It was much more practical than Eloise's loose, dark curls spilling everywhere. Eloise reached over to give her sister's hand a small squeeze of solidarity. While Johanna did not move her hand away, she did not reciprocate.

So, whatever was going on was still going on. Eloise was on her own. She clasped her hands in her lap, squeezing them so she would not shake, and tried not to let her face show the sadness, anxiety, and sheer terror she felt.

Before she knew it, Queen Eloise Hydra Gumball II strode into the Hall of Bald Opulence as trumpets blared a fanfare called "Yo, Yo, Yo, Folks! It's the Queen!" The hall, filled to the walls with hundreds of people, each holding a drum, got to their feet to welcome their monarch. King Chafed followed behind her holding two drums, one for himself and one for the queen. The Queen walked to the center of the dais, stepped up, and turned to face the audience, holding up a hand for silence. The only sound was the scratch of the Court scrivener's quill against hemp parchment. She let the moment hang, then issued the traditional greeting of "G'late-afternoon, my friends!"

"Our queen!" came the familiar response.

"Please be at rest." Drums clattered, clothing rustled, and chairs scraped as everyone sat.

"There has not been a Thorning Ceremony in these halls for a generation. Unfortunately, we must start this rare event on a sad and somber note, acknowledging the passing of Baroness Sÿlvia Nûûûttëëërlïïïng Stúúùbenhocker née de Gumball, one of the greatest Thorning Masters the realms have ever seen. She served well over 100 years, and left her lasting mark on many a high noble lass. Her body is now making its way to her birthplace, Look Elsewhere For A Place To Claim Land You Intruding Amateurs These Hills Are Mine, where she'll be laid to rest in her family's crypt. Let us have 83 seconds of silence in her memory."

The scribe flipped over a gilded deathglass, a slim, single-purpose, ornate hourglass used to time the correct length of memorial silence.

Head bowed, but eyes up, Eloise took the opportunity to scan the crowd. Lots of familiar faces. Whether they expected it or not, they would witness her humiliation. Eloise had settled on a simple strategy: go ahead with the ceremony, continuing as long as she could, and then deal with the consequences when she inevitably broke down, fainted, or collapsed in a heap.

She spotted Jerome sitting in the front row, toward the side, next to his mother, Seer Maybelle de Chipmunk. Eloise was glad he was there. He caught her eye and gave her a thumbs-up. She smiled. At least someone was on her side.

When the sands had fallen through the deathglass, the scribe coughed slightly and the queen continued. "Let us begin. Please rise for the Venerable Prelate Herself."

The room rose as one, and the Venerable Prelate Herself waddled her way from the back of the room. Eloise suspected she did this on purpose to remind people how important she was. The tapir held her short snout piously in the air, like she was ready to sniff out the Divine One should the occasion arise. At long last, she reached the dais, stepped up, and settled on her haunches so she could gesture with her forelegs. "Çalaht be with us," she wheezed.

"Çalaht be with us," replied everyone in unison, habit learned from years spent at devotional houses.

"May we all be graced by Her gap-toothed smile."

"Gap-toothed smile."

The Venerable Prelate Herself launched into an extended homily about something that was presumably relevant, though Eloise could not say what. She had trained herself years ago to tune out the Venerable Prelate Herself when she was sermonizing. Inevitably, toward the end, she said, "So, in short..." and Eloise had found that if she listened to what came after that, she got the gist well enough to hold her own in any discussion afterwards.

Her mind must have wandered, because she suddenly heard, "So, in short, that is why the purity shown by sponges, loofas, and Porifera in general is a perfect example of Çalaht's intentionality, especially, vis-à-vis, our fellow travelers in the realm of spirit. Here endeth the homily, especially for the Thorning Ceremony."

Eloise had no idea what that meant. Maybe she should have paid attention. The Venerable Prelate herself went back onto all fours, turned toward the twins, and waved a four-toed front foot in their general direction as benediction. She then bowed to the queen, relinquishing proceedings back to her.

There was an audible sigh of relief in the room. Eloise hoped the Venerable Prelate Herself did not take offense at that, although she guessed the cleric was either too deaf or too proud to hear it, or was used to it by now.

Queen Eloise returned to the dais. "Next, I would like to welcome the new Thorning Master for the Western Lands and All That Really Matters, Märgärët von den Kleiderschrankbenutzer."

The trumpeters blew a familiar, welcoming fanfare called "Holy Crud, This Is So Exciting!" followed immediately by the more somber, "This One Has No Name, But It Sure Sounds Important." As the music blared, Märgärët stepped out from behind a curtain and walked toward the front. She wore the deep-black-veiled dress of her new position, an outfit similar to the baroness's, but made contemporary with more flattering sleeves, collar, and cut. She was no longer the servant, so no longer dressed as one.

The Thorning Master reached the front and lifted her veil. Eloise gasped. Märgärët's face, neck, and hands were all marked by new piercings. Drops of blood and serum seeped from dozens and dozens of the fresh wounds. The design was similar to that which the baroness had worn, but Märgärët had patterned them in a combination that better suited her sharper, younger features, and which personalized their symbolism. The changed look was striking, fearsome, and breathtaking. No wonder she had said it would take her three days to prepare. She would have done all of that on her own.

"Thank you, Queen Eloise." Her voice slurred a little—the result of the still-unfamiliar tongue piercing, Eloise guessed. The baroness had had one, too—perhaps it was required by the role, or traditional somehow. Beyond this impediment to speech, Märgärët's voice also cracked and her hand shook, her nervousness showing.

Märgärët motioned to the table and three chairs on the dais. Two of them faced the room, and one was on the opposite side. Eloise walked over and stood behind the right-hand chair, leaving Johanna the one on the left.

The new Thorning Master faced the crowd. "I declare the Thorning Ceremony has begun. Please rise." She picked up a rattle from the table, a cylinder of wood with decorative beads strung around the outside. She raised both hands in the air, holding the rattle aloft in one, and faced the direction of the morning sun. Everyone in the room stood with her, also holding up their hands.

With five sharp shakes of the rattle, Märgärët began a variation of a benediction once recited by Çalaht herself. "To those of the east who came before us, we invite benevolent spirits to join us today and witness our ceremony. Teach us to perceive with your discernment, and grace us with your wisdom. Ancestors all, so be it."

The crowd, who also had both hands high, echoed the last sentence. "Ancestors all."

She made a quarter turn widdershins and shook the rattle five times. "To those of the north who came before us, we invite benevolent spirits to join us today and witness our ceremony. Teach us to journey with your openness, and grace us with your stamina. Ancestors all, so be it."

"Ancestors all."

Another quarter turn and rattle. "To those of the west who came before us, we invite benevolent spirits to join us today and witness our ceremony. Teach us to learn with your eagerness and grace us with your curiosity. Ancestors all, so be it."

"Ancestors all."

"To those of the south who came before us, we invite benevolent spirits to join us today and witness our ceremony. Teach us to act with your surety and grace us with your judgment. Ancestors all, so be it."

"Ancestors all."

Next, she squatted, put a hand on the stage, and rattled earthward. "To those of the earth who came before us, we invite benevolent spirits to join us today and witness our ceremony. Teach us to honor the land below our feet and grace us with your support and care. Ancestors all, so be it."

"Ancestors all."

Lastly, she stood again, looked upward, and rattled. "To those of the sky who came before us, we invite benevolent spirits to join us today and witness our ceremony. Teach us to let our minds soar and grace us with your willingness. Ancestors all, so be it."

"Ancestors all."

The blessing of directions gave Märgärët time to settle into her role, and Eloise heard the growing certainty in her voice with each stage of the ritual. The Thorning Master walked to the dais, where the Thorning Ceremony section of the *Livre de Protocol* was open and waiting. Ignoring the rantings of the Elfrics Elder and Younger, Märgärët recited the lines codified in the two-handled scroll. "Ye shall pierceth the flesh—scalp, face, neck, and hands—of the most honored maidens, and name from among them the Heir." The new Thorning Master paused. "Let us now start. Please be seated, and ready your drums."

❧ 28 ❧

THE THORNING CEREMONY

A rustling murmur filled the hall as everyone positioned their drums, beaters at the ready. At a gesture from the Thorning Master, the girls sat and Queen Eloise struck the first notes, leading everyone in a slow, two-beat cadence. With scores of drums in an enclosed room, the sound was thunderous. They settled into a thump-thump, pause, thump-thump, pause, thump-thump—a languid beating of the heart. Eloise found it comforting in a way she had not expected. The drumming enveloped her, vibrated through her, and she relaxed into its monotony.

Märgärët took her chair opposite the girls, her back to the crowd. She removed two tied bundles from a pouch slung over her shoulder and put one in front of each. At her nod of permission, Eloise loosened the black ribbon that held her bundle closed, and unrolled it to reveal a new set of thorns—only 14. The mad monk's breakfast thorns were still not there. Those that lay before her now looked familiar, but different. Fresher, maybe.

"Behold, the thorns of the Thorning Ceremony." Märgärët spoke to the princesses, but her voice carried to the corners of the room. Her phrasing was timed to fit between the languid drumbeats. "These

143

thorns were gathered for this specific day. I, personally, picked some of them. Others I chose from parcels sent here on your behalf. Are you ready to begin?"

Johanna nodded immediately, and placed her hands flat on the table, ready to start.

Eloise hesitated, took a breath, then nodded as well, thinking that the sooner they started, the sooner she'd be done with the whole thing.

Märgärët reached into her pouch again and pulled out two hourglasses. These were slightly larger than the deathglass, but small enough to be used as kitchen timers. She put one in front of each girl. "When your thorn is placed, I will turn over your timer. You must wait until the top chamber is fully spent before you place the next thorn. That will help ensure that you enjoy the full benefit of the process. I will confirm when the time is right for you to continue. Understood?"

They nodded.

Next, she took out two small mirrors, one for each of them. "This is to help you be true with your aim. I encourage you to use it, especially with the later thorns, when your..." Märgärët paused, searching for the right word. "Your capacity is likely to diminish. Understood?"

Again, the two girls nodded.

"Good. In your own time, you may place your first thorn."

There were two things that Eloise had thought a great deal about in the previous couple of weeks: where she would place the thorns if she could actually do it (Plan A), and what she would do when faced with the reality of the ceremony (Plan B). She did her Plan A thinking because Baroness Stúüùbenhocker had made it part of their training. She did her Plan B thinking out of desperation and necessity. Plan A incorporated Plan B, more or less, but the former was more interesting to contemplate, and involved less fighting down of panic.

Which is exactly what she started feeling as soon as Märgärët told them they could start.

Eloise picked up her first thorn and showed it to the Thorning Master, who called out, "Thorny olive," so everyone would know. "And Çalaht's knitter." Johanna was going straight for one of the hardest ones. So be it. Eloise wasn't going to compete. She couldn't. She used some of the iron ring training to block out the rest of the world and concentrated on what she needed to do.

"The thorn has been placed," said Märgärët. She reached over, upended Johanna's hourglass, and sand began draining. Eloise glanced at her twin. The Çalaht's knitter hung from her temple. Ouch.

Eloise didn't have the mental space to wonder about the symbolism of Johanna's placement, but intuitively, it struck her as odd. She opened up the palm of her left hand, studied it for no more than a second, then jabbed the thorny olive into the middle of it. The thorn, being fresh, went in easier and deeper than expected, which meant it hurt more than Eloise was ready for.

Märgärët flipped the hourglass, saying, "The thorn has been placed."

Eloise hoped the symbolism would be clear enough—connection to the earth with her hands. It was an obvious choice, and one she suspected Johanna would also make.

The desire for olives flooded through her, overpowering the itchiness caused by the thorn. The craving was much stronger than it had ever been with her practice thorns. By Çalaht's gnarled earlobes! Eloise felt that if she didn't have olives right then and there, she would burst! *Olives. Olives. Olives. Olives! Olive torte. Olive soup. Olive bread. Olive pasta. Olive relish. Olive garnish. Olive cream pie. Olive slurry. Green olives. Black olives. Olives with pimento in them. Olives with almonds in them. Olive birthday cake.*

If there hadn't been hundreds of people looking at her, she'd have bolted for the kitchens, fallen to her knees, and begged Chef to let her dive into the olive barrel.

Unlike during training, there was no thwack of a bamboo switch to bring her back. Eloise knew she had to control herself on her own. She had experience with this from controlling her habits and knew that she had to distract herself somehow. Eloise pushed aside the olive mania and stared at the draining hourglass to focus her mind away from the cravings. Despite a lingering phantom olive smell lurking in her nostrils and an intense desire to scratch, Eloise was able to wait it out.

As the sands ran out on Johanna's, then Eloise's timer, Märgärët said, "You may proceed with the next thorn when you are ready."

Eloise picked up a choke lily thorn and rolled it between the fingers of her right hand. It was a bit bigger than their practice ones, but not overly.

Märgärët called them out. "Barking vine lotus. Choke lily." And then almost immediately, "The thorn has been placed." She reached for Johanna's timer.

Eloise looked at her sister. The barking vine lotus dangled from her wisdom eye. What was that supposed to mean? Ability to see spirits? Plus, how would she get the thing off?

Not Eloise's problem.

Eloise picked up the mirror and aimed the choke lily at the forward left side of her neck. It was an ambiguous choice, which she hoped would symbolize fluidity in her approach to things (as opposed to being stiff-necked). *Here goes nothing*, she thought, and went for it.

Like the thorny olive, the choke lily thorn was fresh and ready to pierce. It went into her neck easily and deep, and she saw a trickle of blood escape around it. Eloise fought off an urge to swoon.

"The thorn has been placed." Timer flip.

The thirst hit her like a desert taking over her body. Dryness stretched from the back of her throat to the inside of her nose. If she thought the craving for olives had been bad, this was ten times worse. But so was thinking about olives again. Maybe someone could bring her some olive water. Eloise ran her tongue around the inside of her mouth. It was like scraping with sand. What would it be like when the second choke lily went in?

Eloise tried to swallow, but there was nothing there. She tried to imagine sucking on lemons and got the tiniest bit of saliva happening. That made her want lemon-olive cordial, if such thing could be invented. She could invent it. People would love it!

Focus. She needed to focus. More stupid iron-ring staring at the hourglass. More listening to the drums. She still had 14 thorns to go. How could she possibly make it to the end?

After what seemed like a lifetime of olivey thirst, Märgärët said, "In your own time, continue."

Johanna picked up a dervish elder, and Märgärët announced it. A few seconds later, it was placed—back right side of the neck—and Märgärët flipped her timekeeper.

Eloise hadn't even picked her next thorn yet. Should she compound the olive craving or the thirst? Or should she take a pass that round and go for a deadman's bush?

She went for the olive. Eloise raised the thorny olive and, following her plan, placed it in her right cheek. The symbolism she was going for was a bit wafty, but she hoped it would be seen as a cheeky earthiness, although that seemed a bit literal.

Eloise was unprepared for how easily the thorn pierced her cheek—incredibly, it went all the way through. She could feel the tip of the thorn with her choke lily-dried tongue. It made both her cheek and that spot on her tongue itch. Eloise had no idea a tongue could itch so badly. As a renewed, intensified desire for olives washed through her every pore and muscle (*olive tea, olive juice, olive toast*), Eloise panicked at what she had done to herself. She fought the urge to yank the thorn out, knowing she'd just have to put it back. Was there a rule against pulling out a thorn? (*Olive muesli, olive baklava, braised olives in olive oil, boiled olives in olive-flavored water*) No one had said that they couldn't, and if it was in the *Livre de Protocol* or Commentaries, she hadn't seen it.

Wait! The record of her mother's second try at the ceremony mentioned her removing thorns. Then again, that might not be the best example to model. *She must, must, must find a jar of those sweet, giant Shekel olives grown at the foot of the Shekel Mountains in the Eastern Lands. She could practically taste them. Those. Were. The. Olives. She. Had. To. Have. Right. Now!*

Eloise slid the thorny olive back out of her cheek part of the way. It left the metallic taste of blood seeping into the parched wasteland that was her mouth. The itching of her tongue lessened, but lingered.

She'd been too preoccupied to hear, "The thorn has been placed" or see the hourglass flip. So when the Thorning Master said, "In your own time, you may continue," it took Eloise by surprise. That left the second choke lily and the two deadman's bush thorns. The Çalaht's knitter, dervish elder, firethorn, and barking vine lotus were beyond her, which meant she didn't have to worry about the mad monk's breakfast, since she'd never get there.

Given how hard this was so far, she thought she had better save the deadman's bush for last. Besides, how much more thirsty could she feel?

"Choke lily. And choke lily," said Märgärët. Eloise had been too wrapped up in her own experience to think much about Johanna. It was no surprise that she was still going.

It took Eloise a moment to remember where she intended to put the second choke lily—back right side of her neck, opposite the first one. She held the mirror at an angle so she could see what she was about to do, and, being more careful than she had been with her cheek, slid the thorn into place.

She must have hit a nerve bundle, because pain tore through her neck. *Çalaht burning braided bread buns on a brazier*, she managed not to scream. *That hurts!*

The two choke lilies combined to make Eloise feel like all the fluid in her body had dried in the hot summer sun. She was a parched husk, a pot boiled dry, a desiccated, itching, olive-yearning crust left to wither in the dry winds of a wasteland. She realized that it was just a mind trick, an illusion conjured by some property buried in the thorns. But the thirst was her complete reality and her everlasting future. That made her inexplicably sad. Sad, desperate to scratch, and furiously yearning for olives.

Through the fog of all-consuming dryness, Eloise thought about how her language seemed to be missing a word. There was a word for dying due to lack of food—starvation. But there was no word for passing away from lack of water. "Dehydrate" wasn't quite right. It got the dry bit, but not the death bit. Could you say, "She thirsted to death?" or "She dehydrated to death?" Eloise was thinking she might have to invent the word. That made her wonder who was in charge of coming up with new words, because surely *someone* was in charge of such things. Was there a review committee? Did you have to make a formal submission? Defend your new word in some way, like a scholar defending a scholarly work?

There was a corner of her brain that recognized she was raving. She thought that if she could have looked at herself from the outside, she'd just see a 14-year-old girl staring mindlessly at a hand mirror. The intense desire for olives and water would be invisible.

Märgärët snapped her fingers in front of her face, cutting through Eloise's reverie. "I said that the thorn has been placed, the sands have run down, and you may continue. Do you understand me? Can you hear what I'm saying?"

Eloise nodded, recalling herself to the moment. She was in the Throne Hall, not in front of the Committee for Consideration and Approval of Additional Words. The room thrummed with the sound of drums. She needed to collect her wits and stick another thorn into herself.

This really is a stupid ritual. What's the point?

The point, she thought, was that it was a rite of passage. Different peoples, especially warriors, had long undergone rites of passage involving things that might look stupid—scarification, jumping off things, having bits cut off, or being hauled up by ropes attached to skewers through one's chest. At least she didn't have to do that.

Inside Eloise, something suddenly budded. A small, unfamiliar something. It was a desire—a nascent desire to actually get through this thing. Somehow.

Eloise looked at herself in the hand mirror, and at the thorns sitting in front of her. *It's just numbers*, she thought. She was a quarter of the way there. If she placed the deadman's bush thorns, she'd be more than a third of the way there. Maybe there was a way to keep going. She couldn't focus on all of them. That was too overwhelming. But if she could get halfway, then it was just a step to two-thirds.

Maybe she could do this. And maybe she wanted to do this.

Maybe.

Eloise picked up the deadman's bush thorn, waited for Märgärët to announce it, then put it in her right temple. Instantly, that part of her face went numb. A few drops of blood dripped onto the table, but Eloise had not felt them on her cheek. Like the other thorns, these were fresh and potent. If only they could all be that easy, that painless.

That's when the metaphorical candle flame lit over her head.

She had an idea.

✣ 29 ✣

PORCUPINE-ISH

The idea was so simple.

As soon as Märgärët said, "You may continue in your own time," Eloise picked up two thorns, a firethorn and the other deadman's bush. Märgärët announced them, a question mark in her voice. Eloise put the latter into her left temple, and a second or two later, when it was numb, she pushed in the firethorn. Symbolism: who cared. No searing pain, no burning. Eloise knew as soon as she removed the deadman's bush that the thing would hurt like a black-smith's tongs pulled from a forge, but at least it was in there. Märgärët flipped the hourglass, giving her a sidelong look.

Eloise waited for the sands to fall. The drumming sped up, no longer a leisurely heartbeat. Now it was the pace of a brisk walk. The vibration of it thrummed through her, buzzing her body with sound.

"You may proceed in your own time."

Eloise gripped the second firethorn, and put it in her right temple, already nicely numbed. With the two firethorns and the two deadman's bushes poking from her temples, Eloise thought she looked rather porcupine-ish.

When Märgärët announced the placing and flipped the glass, her manner had turned dubious. "You may proceed in your own time."

Eloise picked up a dervish elder spinner, and while the Thorning Master announced it, she pulled out the deadman's bush from her right temple and placed it in a spot on her neck. The numbness in her temple receded, and the firethorn filled it with burning. Eloise did what she could to ignore it and placed the spinner next to the deadman's bush. Not only did it make it possible for her to pierce herself, but it kept the dervish elder's dizziness at bay.

Eloise looked up and saw Johanna staring at her. *That's cheating*, her sister signed, furious.

Based on what?

Based on... Based on... everything! Johanna looked at Märgärët. *She's doing it wrong. Tell her!*

In her pique, Johanna had forgotten that only Eloise would understand their signing, Nonetheless, Märgärët got the gist. The new Thorning Master paused, considering the situation. Baroness Stúüùbenhocker would have known what to do, There was a sudden, unexpected sadness on Märgärët's face. She closed her eyes like she was consulting the Unseen, the way Seer Maybelle did. Eloise guessed she was actually consulting a memorized portion of the *Livre de Protocol*. She stood and stepped to the two-handled scroll she'd read from originally. Märgärët picked up the reading pointer and leaned in to consider the text and commentaries. The drumming faltered, but she looked up and motioned to keep it going.

She considered the text for a full five minutes. For Eloise, they were five long, itchy, burning, olive-filled minutes that she'd rather not have spent. When Märgärët returned to her spot at the table, she said, "There is nothing that forbids this approach. I personally don't think it particularly in the spirit of the undertaking, but I cannot see how I can disallow it. The scribe can note it however she wants. You may continue in your own time."

Johanna was incensed. She liked rules, and this appeared to be breaking them. She straightened her back, turned her attention forward, and proceeded the same way she'd been going before, thorn by thorn, as tradition had it.

Eloise didn't care. She'd found an approach that worked for her, more or less. The numbing effect of the deadman's bush was temporary. If the point was to suffer, she was still suffering plenty, and would continue to do so. But it was suffering engaged on her own terms. She was doing it her way.

Using the deadman's bush to prepare the areas, Eloise went past the halfway point and kept going to two-thirds. A barking vine lotus on the neck. The other coming out of her crown. A Çalaht's knitter through the palm of her right hand, and the other through her other cheek. She felt the effects of each—the thirst, the dizziness, the hunger for olives, the itch, the burning, the simple pain. As she made it to ten, then twelve, thorns, the drums filling the hall accelerated to a frenzy. Eloise's body caromed from sweat to dryness, from slack acceptance to tense resistance. She transcended her proclivities, her habits, her inclinations. She let herself go, lost herself to the sensations that racked her body and buzzed her mind.

Every now and again, she took a glance at her sister. Johanna fought through her thorns with grim determination, lost to the world around her. Eloise knew she must be feeling all the same sensations, but her blank face did a better job of masking them.

The two girls kept pace with each other. Now that Eloise had found a way to cope, she could place hers faster than her sister. She caught up, and then moved ahead, forcing Johanna to keep up.

When the fourteen thorns were done, their timers ran out at almost the exact same moment. Johanna's was perhaps a sneeze's length ahead. Märgärët motioned for them both to stand. Trying not to jostle the thorns in her palms, Eloise braced herself on the table edge and rose, shaking. Dizziness spun her head, threatening to whoosh her headlong to the ground, but she forced herself to focus on a single spot at the far end of the hall, where a shaft of light from the rising moon did its best to illuminate a sliver of tapestry. Eloise remained upright.

She had done it. She had placed all 14 of the thorns. She had not fainted. She had not cried (that she knew of). She had not taken three separate attempts, like her mother. She had made it this far—much further than she had ever dreamed possible.

Eloise fixed her gaze on the shaft of pale light, iron-ring-staring at it so her attention did not go to her pain and discomfort. The tapestry depicted Çalaht holding the heart of a pirate. It was a somewhat obscure story about Çalaht trying to heal a fatally wounded pirate by putting his heart back in, after it had been ripped from his chest by soldiers while pillaging (who, exactly, was doing the pillaging was never clear).

Eloise had spent plenty of time as a girl sitting in front of the tapestry, wondering about it. It was one of her father's favorites, probably because there were all kinds of king jokes woven into both the tapestry and the story. She'd listen as her dad recounted the tale, groaning when he described how the pirate feels disheartened at what happened to him. He's heartbroken at being dead. He gives the Divine One heartfelt thanks for bringing him back from the afterworld. He calls her his sweetheart. At one point, he even says, "Aye aye, me hearties," although Eloise could never find that actual line in the *Scrolls of Çalaht*. The story was perfect for her father, which was probably why he'd had the tapestry placed so prominently in the Hall of Bald Opulence. That, and the fact that it was baldly opulent.

To frantic drumming, Märgärët had them hold their arms out wide and slowly turn a full circle so all could see the thorns. They continued to affect them at full strength. If Eloise swallowed, she could feel the ones in her neck move. When she moved her head, they resisted and tugged. Her tongue still itched at the spot where the one had gone through, and the tang of blood was still there. Her hands, face, and neck dripped blood, the real-life analog to the drops she'd seen in the drawing on Johanna's scroll.

The Thorning Master reached into her pouch and drew out two stop-pered vials, holding them up for all to see. "Mad monk's breakfast," she called, barely audible above the din. She gave one to Eloise and the other to Johanna, then had them sit back down. "You may continue in your own time."

Eloise's hands shook with pain and she had difficulty unstoppering the vial. She'd thought long and hard about where she would put these. Originally, she figured the wisdom eye would be a good, safe, symbolic thing to do—opening up to wisdom or some such. Then she wondered if the crown of her head would be better—a symbolic connection to the spirit world. She could split the difference and put one in each, which also seemed a pretty safe choice. For a while, she'd considered her temples, but she thought that would just induce headaches.

Eloise looked up, and once again saw the tapestry. Çalaht holding the pirate heart in her holy hands with those weirdly long thumbs.

Heart.

Eloise took that as some sort of sign. *Stuff the wisdom eye and the crown.* She pulled forward the neck of her dress and reaching in, aimed the full potency of both mad monk's breakfast thorns at the middle of her sternum, piercing the skin at her heart.

Reading through the histories of Thorning Ceremonies had given her an intellectual understanding that the mad monk's breakfast might do odd things to her. Princesses before her had sobbed, giggled, become catatonically unresponsive, and run screaming from the room. One had literally climbed the walls. Another had hung from a chandelier. Princess Sally Oblique Castor Gumball had allegedly levitated, but that struck Eloise as unlikely, unless a weak magic for it had somehow been triggered during the ceremony. She had wondered what strange sensa-tion would consume her when the time came. Giggling would have been OK with her. Stunned curiosity would also be fine. The levitating would have been fun. Uncontrolled sobbing was not high on her list, but she would have tolerated it.

But Eloise was unprepared for the strange, all-encompassing sensation that flowed into her as the mad monk's thorns induced their changed state.

She felt love.

𝕏 30 𝕏
ONE HEART OPENS, ONE HEART CLOSES

A sense of expansiveness, an openness, filled Eloise. She looked up and saw the room packed with drummers as if for the first time. She faced the people in the hall, getting a feeling for them, and then extended that feeling to those beyond the castle walls. So many people. Nobles and servants, soldiers and merchants, courtiers and crofters, weavers and ragpickers—all of them people who, Çalaht willing, might one day call her "queen" and allow her to rule them. She felt a bond forming with them, all of them, high-born, low-born, prelate or pauper. A warmth. A palpable connection. She saw herself at the center of everything, strands of light shining out from her heart, amplified by the mad monk's breakfast thorns, joining her to every other heart in the room and in the realm.

The love was all-encompassing, vast, deep, and filling.

Tears came. Not from pain, but from an overwhelming sense of oneness. These people would never know her. Never truly. They would not know her quirks and her imperfections. They would judge her, gossip about her, write down her words, decisions, and deeds, and—if she did a particularly good job or a particularly bad one—remember her, more or less, when she was gone. What Eloise felt in this moment of union was that when her time came, she would work to be worthy of it all. Silently, she promised that her manner, choices, and actions would honor the light-filled connections she felt at that moment, even when what she was experiencing had faded to dull memory.

Märgärët saw the radiance that filled Eloise and the palpable love pouring from her. In all her studies with the baroness, the records she'd read and the conversations they'd shared, she'd never heard of one who took this particular path at their Thorning Ceremony. It was in this moment that Märgärët truly became a Thorning Master, recognizing not just the completion of the ceremony's journey, but the transformation it engendered. This was a princess who would someday deserve her crown.

Märgärët raised both hands above her head, crossing her arms and drawing all eyes to her. The drumming sped up, growing impossibly fast and loud. With a sharp motion, the Thorning Master threw her arms wide, and as one, the drumming stopped. There was a lingering echo, then silence. At her cue, the musicians played a fanfare called "Well, That Was Something, Wasn't It?"

Voice stronger than ever, the Thorning Master turned to the queen. "Queen Eloise, I declare that the ceremony is done, and the task completed by the firstborn. Your declaration may proceed." Then she remembered Johanna. Märgärët flicked her eyes to where she sat next to her sister. The young woman's expression was dark, her cheeks flushed, her jaw clenched, and she shook. The Thorning Master added, "It has also been completed by the second born."

Queen Eloise nodded to the Thorning Master, raised an upward palm at a Court herald, and said, "Please."

The herald stepped forward. "Ladies and gentlemen of all species, I present to you the Future Ruler and Heir to the Western Lands and All That Really Matters, Princess Eloise Hydra Gumball III!"

The room erupted in cheers. "To the Princess! To the Princess!"

Eloise stood, legs unsteady and walked as carefully as she could to the center of the dais. Slowly, she curtsied, head down. She saw blood drip onto the dais. Her blood. Her life force. She had spilled it, willingly, in the end, for those who would one day be her subjects. And she loved them all.

⚜

JOHANNA WATCHED HER SISTER CURTSY TO THE ROOM, AND silently raged. She suspected that much of the furore she felt was the result of the mad monk's breakfast poked into her crown where a firethorn already resided. But whatever the cause, she was definitely livid.

The Thorning Ceremony had been much harder than Johanna had expected. She'd grown to hate the thorny olives and their disgusting cravings—she'd never liked olives, so this was a particular torture. That, plus the dizziness from the dervish elder spinners, had almost caused her to empty her stomach. Still, she'd gotten to the end, and her final hourglass turn had finished two or three seconds before Eloise's. Not that it mattered—but it mattered to her. She'd "won," if only by a hair.

The thing Eloise had done with the deadman's bush irked her. For one, it really did seem like cheating, or at least going against the spirit of the thing. For another, it was a clever solution to what had been a massive problem for her sister. Johanna wondered how premeditated it was. Had Eloise played dumb all along, the numbing trick up her sleeve, or had she found inspiration in the moment? Whatever it was, she had to hand it to her sister, which also irked her. Not that she'd ever admit it aloud.

And now, Eloise stood in front of everyone, turning from side to side, a silly, somewhat addled expression on her face, like she'd been imbibing some liquid consolation for the past few hours instead of enduring the pain and humiliation of the ceremony.

Fanfare. Herald. "I present you the Future Ruler and Heir." "To the Princess!"

Well, there it was. Eloise had been named Future Ruler and Heir. La-dee-dah. Johanna looked at her, thinking it had been inevitable. Eloise was firstborn. She'd made it through the ceremony. There it was.

Johanna refused to let herself cry, although that's exactly what she wanted to do. Her being named Future Ruler and Heir had been a long shot. She knew that. But Eloise had been so bad at it all. Johanna had been so much better. It had at least seemed possible.

She'd been kidding herself.

No matter. At least she would get her moment in front of Court. There was that.

Johanna straightened when the first brassy noted played for her. It was a simpler, shorter fanfare called, "Something Else Happened." Johanna tensed. The music was a slight. Perhaps not deliberately so, but anyone who thought about it would realize it was an insult. The Court herald gestured in her direction, and said, "Ladies and gentlemen of all species, I present to you her sister, Princess Johanna Umgotteswillen Gumball!"

"Her sister?" *Her sister!* And even that slap in the face was delivered with a distinct lack of enthusiasm. Similarly, the applause that followed was much more muted, and the smattering calls of "To the Princess" half-hearted.

Johanna's face tightened, then became a rigid blank. She neither bowed nor curtsied. Whatever her expectation was, this was not it. Had she not just endured the same trial? Had she not prepared in the same way? It had been just as arduous, just as much of a challenge to her, and she had borne it well. In fact, better. Less drama. Better adherence to the rules. Faster progress in training. More honor, ability, and willing-ness. No matter how she looked at it, she had done it better.

Better!

These people were blind to that. To them, she was Johanna, second born.

The profound anger she felt found form. It floated down like a dervish elder spinner until it poked its spine into Johanna's gut, sprouted roots, and welled up to fill her soul. Rage. Deep, overwhelming fury.

Johanna gritted her teeth and choked back the feeling. With those half-baked, second-class cheers of "To the Princess," the full impact of being second born settled onto her like a yoke. She would always be seen as second born. Always. Even if her sister died right that second (and she didn't wish that, not even now), Johanna would still be the one who was second born. That was the lens through which people would always see her.

Forever.

This realization, fueled by bitterness amplified by the mad monk's breakfast, ripped something away from Johanna's soul. Fragments of joy, duty, and innocence were pulled from her like handfuls of stuffing and thrown in the air, where they dissipated into nothingness. In their place, hardness formed.

At last, Johanna gave a curtsy—the absolute minimum that met the requirements of Protocol. She righted herself, trained her attention on a far corner of the room where no one was, and focused on that nowhere point like she'd focused on the iron rings of the Torture Tower, blocking out everything else around her.

It really would be a useful practice going forward.

A PLATYPUS AND A DUCK
WALK INTO A ROOM

The rest of the night passed in a blur. The packed crowd made its way to the Culpability Courtyard, where a candlelit celebratory feast was already laid out.

Märgärët took the twins to a side room, where someone had placed two chairs and two mirrored vanities on opposite sides. "Remove the mad monk's breakfast and clean them in the solution," she directed. "Leave the others for the moment."

Eloise wafted over to the vanity on the left and sat. She looked at herself in the mirror. The porcupine-ish look really did not suit her. Eloise wanted to claw the thorns out of her to end the thirst, the cravings, the dizziness, and the burning. Instead, she merely removed the mad monk's breakfast thorns from near her heart. The sense of light and heart connection began to fade, which saddened Eloise. She had hoped the glow would stay with her longer. She set her teeth, and braced herself to tolerate the others.

"You may do with the thorns as you wish," said Märgärët. "I know the baroness would have encouraged you to treat them as a keepsake, but you may not want to. It is up to you."

A herald poked his head in. "The Queen," he announced.

Their mother walked in, and the twins stood and curtsied. "You did well, ladies," she said. It was the first time Eloise could remember her calling them that. It had always been "girls." "There are two things I would like to do," she said, like there was no hurry to remove the thorns at all. "First, I formally end your period of being given over to the Thorning Master. I declare your obligation for silence to be at an end."

"Thank you, Mother," the girls said, almost, but not quite, in unison. The sisters looked at each other, their habit of speaking at the same time suddenly awkward.

"Thorning Master Märgärët von den Kleiderschrankbenutzer, you have done admirably in difficult circumstances. I thank you for your service."

"Thank you, Queen Eloise."

"It is my hope that I shall survive long enough to be in need of your services again for my granddaughters. I enjoin you to study your craft well until then."

"Thank you. I hope to have the chance to serve you again. I will leave you to your daughters." Märgärët curtsied to the queen, then turned to the twins. "It is unlikely I will see you any time soon. Princess, Princess, I thank you."

Eloise wasn't sure what she'd been thanked for, but she curtsied in return, and said, "Thank you, Thorning Master." Johanna simply nodded the minimum allowable nod under Protocol. That surprised Eloise. It wasn't exactly gracious.

As Märgärët left the room, Eloise saw there were two servants waiting in the doorway, a platypus and a duck. Eloise knew them by sight, but had never spoken to either. The queen waved them forward. "I would like to introduce you to your designated handmaids. Eloise, I give you Odmilla de Platypus. Johanna, I present you Nesther de Duck. They have been chosen for you based on their skill, loyalty, compatibility, and trustworthiness. They will come to know everything about you. I assure you, they are worthy of your confidences, and I encourage you to trust them, as I trust mine."

The thought of having a handmaid hanging around, learning all of her habits and proclivities, filled Eloise with low-level dread. But it wasn't like she could say, "I'll give that one a miss, thanks." Being assigned a handmaid was an important step in Court life.

"Odmilla, Nesther, thank you for caring for the princesses. I ask you to treat them with the same care, consideration, and love that has been shown to me by my handmaids."

"Yes, my Queen," quacked Nesther.

"Yes, my Queen," said Odmilla.

Odmilla waddled over on two feet to where Eloise stood by the vanity, and curtsied. "If you please, Princess, it will be my pleasure to serve you." Her rural Southie drawl was one of the heaviest Eloise had ever heard, made more difficult by the rubbery snout. It was certainly one of the most peculiar examples of speech at Court. "If I may, it would be an honor and my pleasure to help with the thorns. I have the Wisdom Salve with me."

"Thank you, Mistress Odmilla. They are driving me spare."

Meanwhile, having bowed to each other without speaking, Johanna and the duck eyed one another, both wary.

"Ladies, I will leave you to it. I have a celebration to attend, as do you," said the Queen. "Take your time. You may join us when you are ready."

"Printhess, if I may." Eloise sat back down and faced the mirror. One by one, Odmilla gently removed the thorns, applying a generous dollop of the wisdom salve to the wounds left behind. The salve was a thick, black paste smelling of turmeric, marigold, aloe, and horseradish. Odmilla was particularly careful with the Çalaht's knitters, applying a bit of salve before she pulled out the serrated thorns, and then adding more when she was done. Eloise did her best not to yell or whimper, but those ones hurt spectacularly. She was especially grateful for the comfort the salve gave when it touched the firethorn punctures, relieving the burning with blessed speed.

Eloise's mirror was angled such that she could see Johanna across the room in profile. Her sister resolutely avoided catching her eye. Johanna had wanted to remove the thorns herself, but Nestor de Duck persuaded her against this. Nesther quacked low words of comfort as she carefully tugged out the thorns. Eloise saw that Johanna allowed herself a few quiet tears, which made her wonder what the handmaid was saying to her.

By the time Eloise and Johanna emerged from the side room and made their way to the Culpability Courtyard, the celebration was in full swing. Eloise had black wisdom salve blotches smeared in 14 visible places and one covered one. Her first inclination had been to wipe them off, but the ongoing relief the salve provided outweighed any vanity. A quick glance showed that Johanna had reached the same conclusion.

Eloise was immediately surrounded by well-wishers, each saying, "Felicitations, Princess, and congratulations to our Future Ruler and Heir." She was lost in a sea of them, and after the trauma of the ceremony and its preparation, their fulsome warmth felt good.

Eventually, Jerome slipped up and handed her a mug of spiced cherry and mint punch. "Felicitations, Princess, and congratulations to our Future Ruler and Heir," he said, although somehow he managed to say it in a way that was more ironic. His voice dropped to a whisper. "Well done, Ellotastic. You had me worried last time I saw you."

"Thanks, Jerome. I'm glad it's a one-off."

He drew a circle around his face. "Nice look, by the way."

"Last thing on my mind. Truly. It feels awesome."

Eloise mingled her way through the crowd, imagining the light bridge between herself and everyone else. She no longer felt it the way she had, but she wanted to retain as much of a sense of it as she could. There was a large part of her that just wanted to escape to her room and curl up with a nice, historical scroll, a cup of haggleberry tea, and a few quarter moon biscuits. But duty was duty, and that meant allowing herself to be congratulated.

An hour and a half later, Eloise saw Johanna by herself, standing under a far arch of the Culpability Courtyard. She looked as stern as Eloise had ever seen her, face devoid of emotion or communication. Eloise set down own her teacup and saucer and signed at her sister. *Felicitations, Jo. Congrats and well done. Are you OK?*

Johanna's face went from stern and disinterested to puzzled. She looked at Eloise like she was confused, shaking her head as if she didn't understand.

I said, congratulations. And are you OK?

Another uncomprehending look. Another shake of the head. This time she added a what-are-you-doing-with-your-fingers motion.

That was odd. *I thought you did well. And I wanted to make sure that you're OK. That's all.*

Johanna gave her an exaggerated palms-upward shrug of complete incomprehension.

Really? What's going on?

Johanna's face suddenly cratered from confused back to stern, and then on to rock-hard anger. Her fingers flashed a quick *I have no idea what you are doing.*

Then she turned her back and looked the other way. Johanna never signed with her twin again.

It broke Eloise's heart.

❧ 32 ❧

EPILOGUE: THREE YEARS LATER

T he almost three years since the Thorning Ceremony had been nothing if not busy.

There had been the funerals, for one. Eloise could represent her mother at funerals. She could show up, convey condolences, and provide that nod of royal attention to the grieving family. Short of falling asleep or getting the name of the dearly departed wrong, it was hard to mess up.

And receptions. So many receptions. Eloise did not mind the fancy frocks and the party food, but she found memorizing all the minor nobility titles, the endless smiling, and having to be nice to people who didn't necessarily deserve it somewhat tiring. Still, they were more fun than the funerals.

But this. This was different. Eloise rubbed a finger along the hem of the Attention Cape, feeling its embroidered edge. She was doing it. She was sitting on the Listening Throne in the Receiving Room for the first time, ready to hear out whoever walked through the door. Maybe it would be a grievance, although she doubted it. Eloise did not have the power to render judgment, so people would know not to bring grievances that day.

Maybe a complaint? She could certainly record a complaint and see that it was passed to the proper person for attention. Although, if she thought about it, a complaint was really a grievance. So, not likely.

The room was empty and had been since she'd arrived. Not even the gossip heralds had bothered to show up. That made sense, since nothing momentous would happen. A junior scribe sat in the corner reading a very legal-looking scroll, though Eloise suspected he had a romance scroll hidden behind it. Which was smart, really—there wouldn't be much other entertainment for him that day.

Läääcy de Aardvark arrived with a steaming pot of haggleberry tea. She smiled at Eloise, poured out a cup, and placed it in its saucer on the table beside the Listening Throne. "You're looking very official today, Princess."

"Thank you, Läääcy. That's very kind."

"Any business?"

"Nope. No customers at all. But, let's be honest—no one really expects anyone to show up today. This is more a practice run than anything else. It's not like I can decide anything."

"Oh, Princess. Don't sell yourself short. Besides, something might happen. You still have a bit of time."

"That's sweet of you, Läääcy, but trust me, I have my expectations appropriately calibrated. Unless someone doesn't read the notice that I am on duty today, I expect the rest of my time will be much like the time until now. Except that now I have a nice cup of tea to occupy me. So thank you."

"Well, Princess, let me know if you'd like anything else." The aardvark tucked the serving tray under an arm, curtsied, and headed back to the kitchens.

The horologist cuckoo called the next quarter hour, then the next, and the three after that. Eloise poured a third cup of tea, pleased it was still hot. One more quarter hour to go, then her time in the Receiving

Room would be done. She didn't mind that nothing had happened. Not really. There would be plenty of times in the future when people would genuinely seek out her ear. It did not have to be now, and for her mother's sake, she hoped it would not be any time soon.

A small, well-dressed figure walked into the room. Eloise straightened so she looked her most capable and sincere. Then she saw who it was: Seer Maybelle de Chipmunk, the Court Visionary.

Odd. Very odd.

Eloise smiled at her. "Seer Maybelle. What a pleasant surprise. You have the honor of being the first petitioner to grace this chamber today. What can I do for you?"

Seer Maybelle stood upright on her hind legs and clasped her claws in front of her. She seemed uncharacteristically nervous. "Princess Eloise, I need to speak with you about my son, Jerome Abernatheen de Chipmunk."

"Yes?"

"Please, please marry my son."

Thank you for reading *The Thorning Ceremony*!

This book is a prequel to *The Purple Haze*, book one in the Western Lands and All That Really Matters series. The Purple Haze starts about three years after this book finishes, and tells the story of Princess Eloise as she sets out on a quest to find her kidnapped sister and bring her back home. Jerome is there with her every step of the way, as is Lorch Lacksneck. It's a rollicking quest full of weak magic, stupidly long names, animals who talk, and wäÿ töö mänÿ ümläüts.

Want to read more about Eloise and Jerome? Six months before the
start of *The Purple Haze*, they
played hooky from Court and headed out for a stolen adventure. It
goes well. And then it really doesn't.
Claim your copy of The Wombanditos today to find out what
happened!

THANK YOU

Thank you for reading The Thorning Ceremony. Reviews are crucial for helping other readers discover new books to enjoy. If you want to share your love for Eloise and Johanna, please leave a review. I'd really appreciate it.

Recommending my work to others is also a huge help. Feel free to give this book and the whole series a shout-out in your favourite book recommendation group to spread the word.

NEXT IN SERIES

AVAILABLE NOW

Her twin abducted. A treacherous rescue mission. Can an unproven princess escape a prophecy of doom?

If you like tongue-in-cheek humor, vivid medieval worlds, and clever cultural references, then you'll love the first book in this lively adventure. *Read The Purple Haze today* (and get it using the QR code below).

NEXT IN SERIES

ACKNOWLEDGMENTS

It is a joy to get to say thank you to those who have helped me bring this book to the world.

Tamsin Dean Einspruch, our daughter, has from the word go been my first port of call for ideas, perspective, and thoughts on words. She is my first reader, and has been with this story every step of the way.

Many, many thanks to Cheryl Hannah and Olivia Martinez for their beta reads. Cheryl and Olivia both brought keen eyes to the words, and provided very different perspectives to what they read. Valuable and valued input all.

Thank you to my editor, Vanessa Lanaway, and my proofreader Abigail Nathan. Y'all rock. It's that simple.

Thank you to Maria Spada for the fantastic cover.

Finally, a huge, massive thank you to my bride, Billie Dean, who reads and gives incredible input on everything I write, who has encouraged me forever, and who believed in my creative soul much, much earlier than I ever did. I love you and I thank you. L^3.

Andrew Einspruch

December 2018

ABOUT THE AUTHOR

Andrew Einspruch is fond of the wordy, the nerdy, and the funny, which means that if you arranged for him to have lunch with Weird Al Yankovic, Tom Lehrer, William Gibson, and any of the Monty Python guys, he'd be your friend forever. Visit his web site for a complete list of his books at andreweinspruch.com.

Andrew is an ex-pat Texan living in Australia, and is the co-founder of the not-for-profit charity the Deep Peace Trust, which fosters deep peace and non-violence for all species. With his wife and daughter, he runs the Trust's farm animal and wild horse sanctuary. (You can see why there's the odd animal or two in his books.)

If pressed, he'll deny he ever coded in COBOL for a bank.

If you haven't done so yet, use the QR code below to claim your copy of the standalone prequel, *The Wombanditos*.

www.ingramcontent.com/pod-product-compliance
Lightning Source LLC
Chambersburg PA
CBHW022000130726

47903CB00014B/2512